The USS Saratoga

(Navy Photo by PH1 William A. Shayka)

The USS Saratoga

Remembering One of America's Great Aircraft Carriers

1 9 5 6 — 1 9 9 4

BY JANE TANNER

LONGSTREET PRESS
Atlanta, Georgia

Published in Cooperation with the Jacksonville Chamber of Commerce

Published by LONGSTREET PRESS, INC.,
a subsidiary of Cox Newspapers,
a subsidiary of Cox Enterprises, Inc.
2140 Newmarket Parkway
Suite 118
Marietta, Georgia 30067

Printed in the United States of America

1st printing, 1994

ISBN: 1-56352-189-X

This book was printed by Horowitz/Rae, Fairfield, New Jersey
Film preparation by Advertising Technologies Inc., Atlanta, GA
Personality profile photos by Diane Uhley

Jacket design by Laura McDonald
Book design by Jill Dible

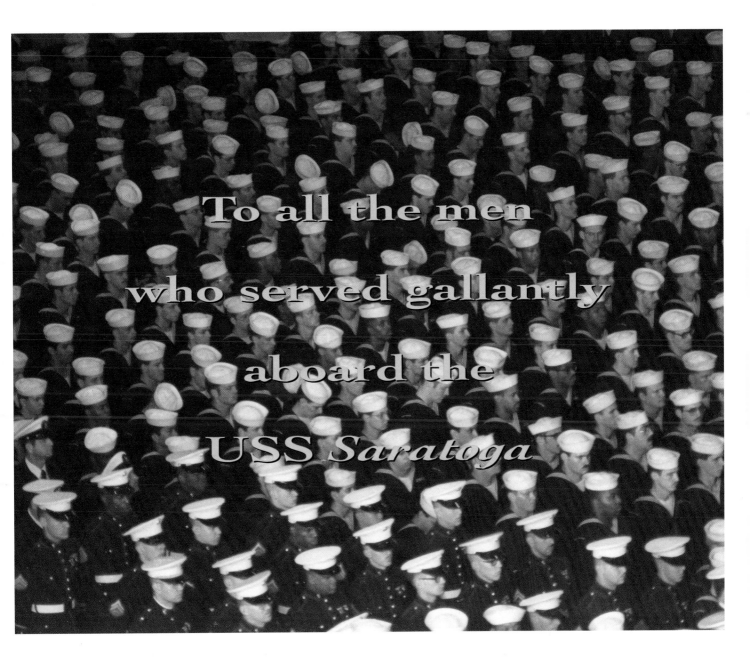

To all the men

who served gallantly

aboard the

USS *Saratoga*

Contents

The crew of the Saratoga *watches an air show in the Mediterranean. (Official U.S. Navy Photo)*

Introduction

This history of the USS *Saratoga* (CV-60) is really 60,000 individual histories written over a period of more than thirty-eight years. Each of the men who stepped aboard the ship found his life indelibly changed by the triumphs and the difficulties. Some came aboard as boys and left as men. Others found new levels of strength and endurance as they mastered difficult and dangerous jobs and acclimated to the crowded, yet isolated life at sea. The gigantic vessel constructed in the 1950s was designed to elevate Navy aircraft carriers to a new level of power, size, and versatility. Operation of the mighty ship and its incessant need for maintenance and repair demanded a great deal from the sailors. In turn, the Navy and its sailors demanded a great deal from the *Saratoga*, as the crew took her on twenty-two deployments to the Mediterranean Sea, a tour in Vietnam, a number of missions into the Red Sea, and exercises in the Norwegian and North seas. Her final mission was in the Adriatic, participating in United Nations operations off the coast of the former Yugoslavia.

In her early years *Saratoga* was tagged a "hard-luck" ship. Even as she first pulled out of the New York Naval Shipyards at Brooklyn, she was plagued with problems in the touted propulsion system. Sailors on other ships parked nearby dubbed *Saratoga* "Building 60" when the ship didn't move for long periods. Despite setbacks, the *Saratoga's* first two decades included participation in the Cuban Missile Crisis, a role in quelling tensions in Lebanon, a return to the Middle East during the Six Day War, and visits by Presidents Dwight Eisenhower and Richard Nixon. While her venue was the Mediterranean, the ship was called to serve in Vietnam and flew nearly 15,000 missions in Southeast Asia.

In the early 1980s, the ship underwent a massive $550 million overhaul. Following the revamping, *Saratoga* participated in the capture of Arab terrorists who had seized an Italian cruise ship and killed an American passenger. Shortly thereafter, she launched strikes on Libya. While ships tend to decline in their later years, *Saratoga* seemed to get stronger and closed with an impressive finish. The ship participated vigorously in the Persian Gulf War and, while stationed off the coast of Bosnia-Herzegovina, played a vital role in U.N. operations to stem Serbian aggression.

Just as important as the high-profile missions, the ship served as a strong presence in the Mediterranean during peace time. The presence of the ship signaled the power and support of the United States and served as a deterrent to would-be aggressors. Europeans became accustomed to the ship's Mediterranean lights, the string of lights aglow from bow to stern as the ship stood off shore at its various ports. Throughout the ship's career, the *Saratoga* promoted cooperation between nations with countless international NATO exercises.

Like any military vessel, the *Saratoga* was

The island of the USS Saratoga. *(Navy Photo by PH1 William A. Shayka)*

marred by a number of tragedies. Pilots were shot down in combat, fierce fires in the machinery spaces and flight deck claimed a number of lives, and a grim ferry accident off Haifa, Israel, killed twenty-one sailors.

Among the thousands who served on the ship over the years were thirty men who started as young Navy pilots and moved swiftly upward through the ranks to command the aircraft carrier. For many, the job as skipper of the *Saratoga* was the step that took them to the rank of admiral. *Saratoga's* commanding officers had the special privilege of watching from the bridge as the colorful, carefully orchestrated flight deck operations launched and landed aircraft more than 300,000 times from the ship.

The decommissioning of the *Saratoga* on August 20, 1994, was a somber and moving ceremony as thousands from her past gathered to say good-bye to the grand carrier that always answered when duty called.

The USS Saratoga

The Saratoga *in New York Harbor in June 1960. (Official U.S. Navy Photo)*

A Thirty-Eight-Year Voyage

On July 23, 1952, orders came through to build the second *Forrestal*-class attack aircraft carrier, part of a Cold War buildup of powerful new Navy carriers. Nine days before Christmas that year, workers at a graving dock at the New York Naval Shipyard in Brooklyn began constructing the keel of CVA-60. During the next three years, 700 engineers, naval architects, and draftsmen poured over 14,000 working drawings while shipyard workers erected 52,000 tons of steel.

The USS *Saratoga* would be "the most powerful vessel ever designed" — even more powerful than her sister ship the USS *Forrestal*, completed shortly before her. The heart of such accolades centered on *Saratoga's* innovative, forceful propulsion system with turbines that would operate at the highest steam temperatures and pressure levels of any ship built for the Navy to date. The modern propulsion design would drive the 60,000-ton carrier at speeds in excess of thirty knots. Its four cross-compound turbines would require less fuel, yet produce greater shaft horsepower. The reduction gears were fifty percent lighter than WWII designs, and were the lightest ever constructed, giving the ship either an increased cruising radius or the capacity for thousands more gallons of aviation fuel than her predecessors. Eight giant oil-fired boilers would provide the steam for her turbines, catapults, and operations. A mighty ship was taking shape.

However, the trumpeted propulsion system would soon prove to be the *Saratoga's* nemesis. Her first commanding officer spent many a restless night with visions of malevolent gremlins working mischief in the engine spaces. Part of *Saratoga's* quickly garnered reputation as a "hard-luck" ship stemmed from such propulsion and engineering problems.

When *Saratoga* was built, it was the largest ship ever constructed in New York. A giant, she struck an impressive pose against the skyline. Nearly five city blocks long and more than a block wide, her flight deck area exceeded four acres. In fact, the *New York Herald Tribune* reported that the first ship named *Saratoga*, 150 tons and built 175

Personnel inspection aboard the Saratoga *in November 1956. (Courtesy of George Tanis)*

years earlier, could be put on the flight deck without seriously interfering with normal operations. Among the flight deck innovations were specially designed angled decks to allow two aircraft to launch simultaneously.

A litany of "gee whiz" facts about the mighty ship filled reports in the press and Navy publications: The ship produced enough horsepower to supply electricity for a city of 1.5 million people. The hangar deck for parking and repairing planes was 2.5 football fields in length. Each anchor weighed thirty tons — each chain link 360

pounds. The length of the anchor and chain ran 2,160 feet. The paint used in construction was enough to cover 30,000 average houses. The ship was equipped with its own full-service hospital and 2,000 telephones amid its 3,000 separate compartments.

But the ship was just inert, cold iron without the men who brought her to life, repaired her again and again, gave her direction, and propelled her over a large part of the world in her thirty-eight-year military career.

Assembling the crew was the job of 41-

year-old Captain Robert Stroh, a New Yorker and a plumber's son who entered Annapolis in 1926. He had been commanding officer of the USS *Valcour* and was executive officer of the USS *Hornet* when it served as a "magic carpet" bringing personnel back from the Pacific at the end of WWII. "*Saratoga* was not completed in late 1955 when I received my orders," recalled retired Vice Admiral Stroh, 87, during a chat in the study of his Jacksonville home. So, during the period from the latter part of 1955 to the early part of 1956, the crew was being assembled in Newport, Rhode Island, by the prospective executive officer, Commander James McCrocklin, and Captain Stroh in New York.

Under darkened skies and intermittent rain showers, nearly 5,000 people gathered at dry dock No. 5 on October 8, 1955. A Navy crane held a canvas over the dais for the VIPs, but the audience had to wrap themselves in raincoats and huddle under umbrellas. Poor weather forced the cancellation of a Navy jet flyover, but spirits weren't dampened. The wife of Navy secretary Charles Thomas was escorted to the bow of the ship. A *New York Herald Tribune* story recounted what followed: "The gates of the drydock opened and water from the East River began to flood in. At the precise moment the entire keel was wet, Mrs. Thomas smashed a bottle of champagne on the bow and said, 'I christen thee *Saratoga*.'"

On January 28, the massive ship was moved 500 yards from the dry dock to Pier Kilo for her fitting-out process. After the lines were cast off at 9:00 a.m., it took twelve tugs about two hours to move the cold iron hulk the short distance. Nearby, on the cold, windy flight deck of the *Essex*-class carrier USS *Leyte*, Captain Stroh watched his ship.

The period in New York leading up to and following the commissioning was exciting for *Saratoga*'s young crew. Those days a military uniform meant free entry to sport and entertainment events, and New York City had plenty to offer. Members of *Saratoga*'s original crew recall walking right into what was then Brooklyn Dodgers Stadium and Giants and Yankees games, and

A Navy recruiting aids facility poster by artist Lloyd Nolan features the Saratoga. *(U.S. Naval Historical Center Photograph)*

Saratoga Vital Statistics

Authorized by Congress	Fiscal year 1953
Keel laid	December 16, 1952
Christened	October 8, 1955
Commissioned	April 14, 1955
Builder	New York Naval Shipyard
Displacement	60,000 standard (78,000 loaded)
Length	990 feet at the waterline
Beam	129.5 feet
Draft	37 feet
Flight deck width	252 feet
Flight deck height	67 feet from the waterline
Flight deck area	176,729 square feet
Hangar deck area	75,052 square feet
Anchors	Two, 30 tons each
Anchor chains	Two, 180 fathoms each
Chain links	360 pounds each link
Catapults	Four, steam powered
Main engines	Four Westinghouse turbines
Boilers	Eight Babcock & Wilson boilers
Shaft horsepower	280,000 horsepower
Speed	30-plus knots
Armament	NATO Sea Sparrow, CIWS, and 75 aircraft
Hospital	64 beds
Telephones	2,300
Number of compartments	1,500
Electrical wiring	10,000-plus miles
Personnel assigned	2,800 (5,000-plus with airwing)
Home port	Mayport, Florida

Source: USS *Saratoga* Public Affairs Office

catching famous performers such as Fats Domino and Chubby Checkers at the lounges along Forty-second Street.

One memory is especially vivid for Russ Doerr, who was a nineteen-year-old storekeeper third class when he reported to the brand new *Saratoga*: "One Sunday night after spending the weekend in New York, everyone was broke as usual. So, we went to the USO at Lexington Avenue and this lady offered us TV tickets. It was for Ed Sullivan, and I said, 'Good, my folks watch it and they might see me on TV.' We had great seats. Third row, center aisle. Ed Sullivan comes out with his arms folded and says, 'Ladies and gentlemen, I've got a special

Vice Admiral Robert J. Stroh (Ret.)

As a young captain, Robert Stroh was the first commanding officer of the USS Saratoga. *He oversaw the assembling of her first crew and the ship's commissioning, and he led the ship on its maiden voyage from the New York Naval Shipyard to Mayport, Florida.*

The commissioning took place on a blustery, cold April morning in New York City. I assembled the crew and, at the proper time, I ordered the crew to break the colors, hoist the colors, hoist the jack, and break the commission pennant, which indicates a ship in commission, an active role. All of this transferred the *Saratoga* to a ship in commission. It becomes a living, breathing, pulsing, vibrant ship with her crew in place, ready to go to sea for the first time.

Our first sortie to sea, we had to pass underneath the Brooklyn Bridge and the Manhattan Bridge with both masts folded down. There was little clearance, particularly under the Brooklyn Bridge. When we passed under the Brooklyn Bridge some of my crew stood on the top levels of the masts and rattled broomsticks against the bottom of the bridge. That's how little clearance we had. But an inch is as good as a foot; so long as we had an inch, that was enough.

I'm still having nightmares over that first sortie down Ambrose Channel because, on the advice of a New York harbor pilot whom I had taken on board, I believed the weather was satisfactory. We unmoored and got underway. Almost immediately after we passed the two entrance buoys, the fog set down to zero, zero. There was nothing to do but keep going. There was no turning, no anchoring in the channel. From the bridge we were blind, so blind that I saw people walking on the flight deck disappear as they headed for the bow.

So I turned the navigation over to my special sea details. I did the praying, and they did the navigation. That's all I could do in a situation like that. We could check off the channel marking buoys as we went by, but it was not until they were almost on our side that we could see the channel buoys. The fog horn was sounding.

I dismissed that harbor pilot. I don't know where he disappeared to, but I never saw him again. We did transit the Ambrose Channel and did clear the lighthouse and found ourselves at sea. For the first time in the history of the USS *Saratoga* [CVA-60], she had deep water under her keel.

The mast of the Saratoga *is dipped to allow passage under a bridge. (Courtesy of Harvey A. Hirsch, Jr.)*

treat for you tonight.' The curtain opens and this guy sings: 'You ain't a nothing but a hound dog, cryin' all the time.' I turn to my friend Wayne and said, 'This guy is never going to make it.' That's the dumbest statement I've ever made in my life. Here we were, Elvis Presley's national television debut."

While there were plenty of distractions in New York, there was plenty of work readying the ship. Alongside the dock, everything that could be tested was tested. Crew members were assigned to duty stations and berthing spaces and began to perform their jobs.

The commissioning ceremony for the $200 million plus vessel took place on a bright but chilly April 14, 1956. Retired Admiral Stroh describes it: "I assembled the crew and, at the proper time, I ordered the

crew to break the colors, hoist the colors, hoist the jack, and break the commission pennant, which indicates a ship on commission, an active role." Not long after Stroh ordered the first deck watch set, forty-six jet fighters zoomed low over a crowded flight deck, according to a report in the *New York Times*. Stroh looked up and announced the flyover as the posting of the aerial watch.

Headlines heralded a great new ship: "Queen of the Seven Seas"; "The Super-Carrier *Saratoga* Captures U.S. Imagination." But debate over the Navy's costly carrier construction program continued in Washington. A *Daily News* column just two days after the commissioning read: "The *Saratoga* cost a fifth of a billion dollars. Is it the best and wisest expenditure of the nation's wealth (and there's limit to every nation's wealth) to spend it on such glorious and impressive aircraft carriers as the mighty *Saratoga* proudly commissioned at the Naval Shipyard, Brooklyn, last Saturday?"

On June 2, the ship left the shipyard under her own power and she passed underneath the Brooklyn and Manhattan bridges with both masts folded down. Hinges to fold the masts were a new aircraft carrier design feature first used on the *Saratoga*. Even with a slack tide, the clearance under the Brooklyn Bridge, the oldest and lowest of the East River bridges, was tight. As the ship passed under, crew members stood on the top levels of the masts and rattled broomsticks against the bottom of the bridge. The ship dominated the harbor, and people came out by the thousands to watch it pass with sailors in full dress blue uniforms on the flight deck. Cars clogged to a stop along nearby streets and bridges, and a train bound for Canal Street slowed to a crawl so passengers could watch the *Saratoga*, according to the *New York Times*.

The ship passed down the East River to Sheepshead Bay and moored to a buoy to take on board 600 representatives from the

On the flight deck October 9, 1956. (Courtesy of George Tanis)

Ike Ayers, Russ Doerr, and Wayne Rickert

Shipmates Petty Officer 3rd Class Russ Doerr, Seaman Wayne Rickert, and Petty Officer 1st Class Ike Ayers were among the original crew of the Saratoga, *reporting to Brooklyn, New York, while the ship was under construction. They all played a part in former president Dwight Eisenhower's tour of the new supercarrier in Mayport in June 1957.*

Russ Doerr was part of a color guard lined up to greet President Eisenhower and got to shake the President's hand.

It is almost unheard of to shoot aircraft off the catapult without it being underway and into the wind. But when Eisenhower's airplane, the *Columbine,* landed, taxied over to the ship and came to a stop . . . the door swung open and, at the exact moment he made his appearance, they shot two jet planes off the bow of the aircraft carrier. You could see that even Eisenhower was taken aback. His face was like, "Oh my god, what was that?" Here these two planes took off. It was something. I was up on the hangar deck and witnessed it. We weren't even aware they were going to do that.

Wayne Rickert carried Secretary of State John Foster Dulles' luggage from the Columbine *to the ship.*

Before Eisenhower came aboard, we had to paint the ship green and white throughout the interior. We spent sixty days at sea doing that. It got so difficult, sailors were getting tired, and they threw green paint over the mascot, the rooster. They took the cock down to the sick bay, plucked out all his feathers, and put talcum powder all over the bird to save it. We still had to keep painting the ship. About a week later, the cage disappeared. I believe it was thrown overboard. Then, the skipper had the entire crew, about 4,000 men, muster on the flight deck. We stood at attention for about four hours in the hot Caribbean sun. The captain came over the squawk box in the observation deck and said he wanted the man who threw the rooster overboard to come forward. No one admitted it. We stood up there until he finally dismissed us.

Ike Ayers was in charge of the detail to get Eisenhower's and his cabinet's baggage from the two planes into the assigned staterooms.

The crew that Eisenhower brought on board, stewards and everyone, brought on board his silverware, his plates, and his food. He did not eat the food on the ship.

[*Ayers had this to say about the green rooster escapade.*] The interesting thing is that when we pulled back into Mayport, some gal in the Mermaid Bar in Jacksonville Beach made up a song that became very popular: "Who Painted the Rooster Green?"

Navy Department to watch the builders' trials. After all, the *Saratoga* represented the next phase in engineering and design. It was a showcase.

The ship's first passage through Ambrose Channel proved to be treacherous because of a heavy fog that shrouded the entire ship. Captain Stroh watched sailors walking a few steps in front of him instantly disappear into the thick white clouds. The New York harbor pilot who had advised Captain Stroh that the weather was fine for moving forward was quickly dismissed. The giant ship couldn't be turned around in the narrow channel, so a special navigation crew used radar to allow her to move forward. The fog horn sounded as the ship crept passed the channel buoys. Captain Stroh held a prayer vigil on the bridge. "We did transit the Ambrose Channel and clear the lighthouse and found ourselves at sea for the first time in the history of the USS *Saratoga*," Stroh recalled. "She had deep water under her keel."

The new crew of the *Saratoga* soon learned that the first attack mission was to go after the gremlins wreaking havoc in the propulsion plant. "Throughout my time on board, we continued to chase gremlins in the main propulsion plant," Stroh said.

When the ship first traveled from New York to what would become its permanent homeport, Mayport, Florida, it didn't stay there long. Stroh wanted to get the ship quickly to the naval base at Guantánamo Bay, Cuba, to work on the propulsion system and conduct the shakedown period and training for the crew and the air group attached to the ship.

Stroh decided it wouldn't be wise to spend too much time at the Florida base where word of the mechanical troubles could leak. After all, this was an expensive taxpayer project with more carriers on the drawing board, and, during the Cold War, information about military hardware was best kept under wraps.

The Mayport and Jacksonville communi-

Captain Robert J. Stroh (right) and Ensign T. F. Rinard display the ceremonial cake for the 1,000th landing aboard the Saratoga. *(Courtesy of George Tanis)*

ties were thrilled at the arrival of the ship. The tenuous survival of the Mayport basin following WWII seemed secured with the arrival of the aircraft carrier. After the war, the base at Mayport was abandoned and given to the Coast Guard. But according to Charlie Bennett, Jacksonville's longtime congressman who was first elected in 1949, even the Coast Guard didn't need it. Bennett was chairman of the sea power subcommittee and helped pass legislation his first year that

Patricia Mehle

Throughout the years, wives and families were an integral part of the success of the Saratoga. Patricia Mehle, wife of Rear Admiral Roger W. Mehle (Ret.), started the first USS Saratoga Officers' Wives Club when her husband took command of the ship in 1960. She was the first commanding officer's wife to meet the ship at foreign ports during a Mediterranean deployment.

*S*ara was scheduled to arrive at the saluting point off Piraeus, Greece, at 8:00 a.m. on the twenty-third of January in 1961. When several hours had passed, it was clear something unusual had occurred. The other wives and I waiting were, of course, very concerned. When she finally anchored and I was able to go on board, I learned of the tragic events of the preceding night. My heart went out to the families of the casualties. I was escorted, at my husband's behest, to the sick bay where the executive officer, Joe Reese, lay seriously ill from smoke inhalation as he slept in his cabin at the outset of the fire. En route to the sick bay, I was appalled to see the extent of smoke damage in officers' country. Grimy, oily deposits were everywhere, resulting from the air conditioning system picking up noxious, heavy smoke from the fire below in No. 2 machinery space. The painful aftermath of the fire, however, seemed to galvanize the entire crew into heroic efforts to erase, where possible, the signs of the fire. Even though *Sara* had lost one quarter of her propulsion plant, officers and men successfully completed the ship's scheduled deployment and met all commitments.

On the lighter side, in Naples, the ship's next port of call, I learned of a needy boys orphanage, Casa Scugnizzi, in which young boys were living in great poverty. Clothing was a principal need, and when I returned to Mayport, the wives' club sponsored a clothing drive for the boys. Hundreds of pounds of clothes were delivered to Casa Scugnizzi on the ship's next deployment with great gratitude from the priests in charge of the orphanage.

My recollections of our relationships with the people of Jacksonville, Mayport, and the Beaches can only be described as wonderful. My time there with the ship was unforgettable.

established Mayport as a major ship port for the Navy.

The *Saratoga* is unique among Navy aircraft carriers of its generation because it remained in the same home port throughout its career. Over the years, strong ties were forged between the ship and the city of Jacksonville and its beach communities. At the time of this printing, a strong community effort was underway to raise enough funds to make the retired carrier into a naval museum in Jacksonville.

On October 24, 1956, an aircraft made the first arrested landing on the *Saratoga*'s flight deck when a Grumman F9F-8 Cougar, flown by CAG-4 Commander William Ely, came down and swept the deck and caught the arresting cable.

After completing the shakedown, the *Saratoga* headed north but was detoured away from Mayport by hurricane-force winds. She stopped off at Norfolk, then moved on to her builder's yard where she stayed from December through February of the next year undergoing repairs and modifications.

PRESIDENT EISENHOWER VISITS THE *SARA*

The biggest event thus far in the young career of the *Saratoga* was the two-day visit of President Dwight Eisenhower and his cabinet. The crew readied for the guests by arduously repainting the interior of the ship, among other preparations. On June 6, 1957, Eisenhower's plane, the *Columbine*,

pulled up next to the *Saratoga* at the base in Mayport. In a dramatic display, two *Saratoga* aircraft forcefully launched off the flight deck as Eisenhower stepped out of his plane. The jet blast impressed, even startled, the president. It was unheard of to launch aircraft while the ship was alongside the dock, as opposed to offshore and heading against the wind. During the visit, the *Saratoga*, along with eighteen other ships, provided demonstrations of air operations, antisubmarine warfare, guided missile operations, and bombing and strafing techniques. "A highlight of the Chief Executive's visit came when two new Vought F8U-1 Crusaders of VX-3 spanned the nation in three hours and twenty-eight minutes, launching from *Bon Homme Richard* (CVA-31) on the West Coast and landing on the *Saratoga* in the Atlantic.

President Eisenhower chats with pilots of the Saratoga *during a two-day visit off the Florida coast, June 6–7, 1957. (U.S. Naval Historical Center Photograph)*

President Eisenhower speaks to Captain Robert B. Moore during his visit to the Saratoga. *(Courtesy of George Tanis)*

Also making the transcontinental flight were two A3D-1's from VAH-9, demonstrating the carrier Navy's nuclear delivery capability," according to *The Hook* magazine (Summer 1980).

In early fall, *Saratoga* began her first trans-Atlantic voyage, heading to the Norwegian Sea to participate in a NATO exercise with more than 100 ships, dubbed Operation Strikeback. For the young crew, it meant pulling into inlets such as the Firth of Clyde and ferrying to shore in whaleboats to visit cities such as Glasgow and Edinburgh. Greatly impressed by the U.S. military visit, people traveled from all

over Scotland to meet the *Saratoga* sailors in Edinburgh. The crew went on to England and France, in what was partly a goodwill mission to show off the newest and largest aircraft carrier in the world.

Following a trip to Norfolk for repairs and a return to Mayport, the *Saratoga* set out February 1, 1958, for the first of what would eventually be twenty-two cruises to the Mediterranean. When the ship arrived at Gibraltar, she took part in Sixth Fleet training maneuvers. It wasn't long before the ship was called to respond to political troubles in the region. A coup in Iraq led to instability in the eastern Mediterranean.

On July 14, much of the crew was on liberty in Cannes, Frances, enjoying Bastille Day events. Harvey Hirsch, a storekeeper on the ship at the time, remembers the liberty was interrupted suddenly by the loud siren, calling the sailors back to the *Saratoga* as quickly as possible. The president of Lebanon, Camille Chamoun, had asked President Eisenhower to help keep the threat of a Syrian invasion at bay. In a matter of hours, CVG-3 aircraft were providing support to Marines landing on the beaches at Beirut. *Saratoga* launched thousands of round-the-clock air support missions over a period of thirty-

one days as part of an American force that quelled a troubling situation in Lebanon. The operation helped dissuade the Syrians from interjecting themselves into Lebanon's political affairs. For two months, the ship remained in the waters off Lebanon, providing photo-reconnaissance and combat air patrol to protect the fleet and personnel on shore.

On her second Mediterranean deployment, the ship took part in a number of NATO exercises with British, French, Greek, and Turkish navies. During the third Mediterranean cruise, while the ship was in the Aegean Sea heading toward Athens, a fire broke out in the No. 2 engine

On the flight deck in October 1961. (Courtesy of Ernie Haakenson)

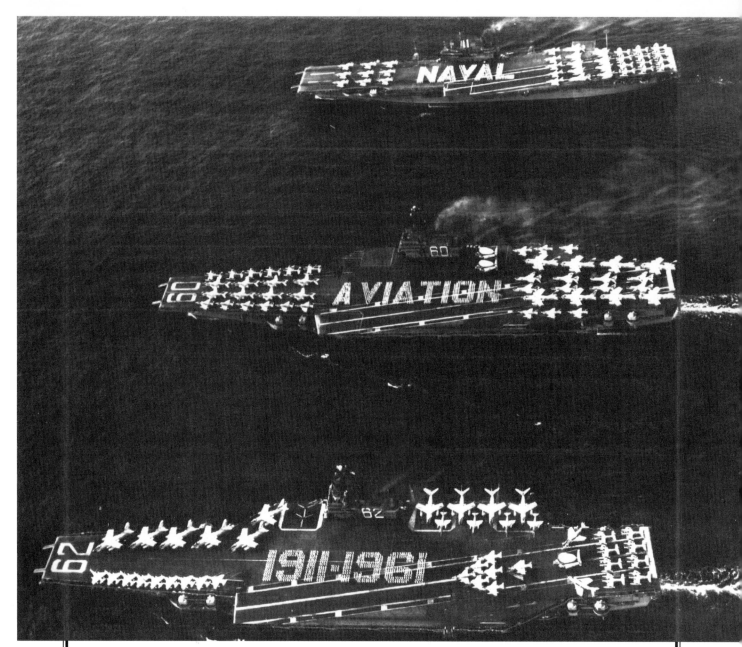

Three of the Navy's finest aircraft carriers celebrate fifty years of naval aviation. From top, the USS Intrepid *(CO Charles Minter), the USS* Saratoga *(CO Roger Mehle), and the USS* Independence *(CO Harvey Lanham). All three commanding officers were part of the class of 1937 at the U.S. Naval Academy, Annapolis. (Official U.S. Navy Photo)*

room. Shortly after midnight on July 23, 1961, watch hands were switching a valve that delivers oil to the high-pressure system. A gasket failed and high-pressure oil spewed against hot machinery and flashed into fire. Retired rear admiral Roger Mehle, the skipper at the time, remembers being awakened just after midnight and rushing to sound general quarters from the bridge.

Initially, it was difficult to stop the source of the fire. Before the men in the control room could close the broken valve to stop the flow of oil, Mehle recalled, smoke billowed in and forced everyone to rush out. Smoke had poured through open port windows between the control room and machinery. The windows had been taken out under a previous command so sailors on watch could hear the machinery grinding and humming to determine if it was operating properly. To make matters worse, the ship's touted air conditioning system was recirculating clouds of smoke laden with oil throughout the ship — even into Damage Control Central. The smoke was so bad in the state rooms below the hangar deck, that Executive Officer Joseph Reese was overcome by smoke inhalation and was taken to the sick bay in serious condition. It took several hours to extinguish the fire. Tragically, seven men died.

A Christmas tree gives the hangar bay a festive atmosphere in 1961. (Courtesy of Ernie Haakenson)

Mehle's wife, Patricia, was waiting at the Athens port Piraeus, wondering why the ship was late. When it arrived at about 10:00 a.m., she quickly went aboard to support the crew. She recalls visiting the executive officer in the sick bay. "He was still covered with soot, his voice was low," she said.

The question now was whether the ship could continue its operation. "There was all kinds of consternation in Washington about whether we could conduct our mission," Mehle recalls. "If we stayed we had to operate on three propeller shafts. Our choices were to stay there or come back with our tail between our legs." The decision: stay. The crew rallied in a massive clean-up effort. By 3:00 p.m., Greek dignitaries were making routine on-board visits.

Mehle is still impressed by the crew's attitude to put the disaster behind them and succeed. After resuming operations with the Sixth Fleet, then going into Norfolk for repairs, the ship conducted refresher trials at Guantánamo Bay and received the highest grade of any carrier in the past decade.

Soon thereafter, on October 25, 1961, an entourage from Washington, D.C., visited the ship to watch air group CVG-3 embark and watch a demonstration of abilities in an air show. Among the guests were men who would all continue to make individual contributions to the country's history: U.S. Attorney General Robert Kennedy, Secretary of Defense Robert McNamara, Secretary of the Navy John Connally, and Byron R. White, assistant to the attorney general.

During the fourth Mediterranean cruise, as was the case during numerous other deployments, *Saratoga* was involved in simulated nuclear strikes. Exercise Big Game involved a joint U.S. and French nuclear strike in the Western Mediterranean, and during RegEx-62 mock full-scale nuclear attacks were made against targets in Italy, Greece, and Turkey.

Captain Roger Mehle holds a Christmastime dinner in the captain's cabin in 1960. (Courtesy of Patricia Mehle)

"On the Line" in Cuba

Saratoga spent a good part of the summer of 1962 at the shipyard in Portsmouth, Virginia, just outside Norfolk. Among other modifications, her angled deck was extended. Flight deck changes were made to allow for newer, heavier aircraft. After U.S. airplanes brought back photographs showing Soviet missiles in Cuba, the shipyard work was rushed. The ship pulled out three weeks ahead of schedule. The normal complement of ammunition was loaded outside Norfolk, but when *Saratoga* got to Mayport, it was decided her aircraft would need different bombs for the Cuba operations. "We swapped low-drag bombs for fat bombs," remembers Paul Stadler, a gunnery officer and department head at the time. The ship moved toward Guantánamo to take its place

"on the line," between December 5 and 15, 1962, in the Cuban Quarantine operations. That same year, the ship was able to enjoy its first Christmas at its home port in four years.

Few work settings in the world are as dangerous as a carrier flight deck: swift, forceful launches, screeching halt landings, explosive fuels, jet blasts and powerful machinery in constant motion. One of *Saratoga*'s worst flight deck fires took place on August 15, 1963, off Sardinia, when an errant aircraft mistakenly landed on the flight deck and crashed into a row of planes being readied for the last launch of the night. Erroneously, the runway center line lights were on; the F3H Demon pilot radioed his approach.

A vivid memory for many of the sailors on the flight deck that night was watching shipmate AMS3 Jack A. Sherrill, Jr., rush to the flight line, stand in the path of the oncoming plane, waving his flashlight director wands to signal away the pilot. The plane struck Sherrill and crashed into a row of planes, igniting a series of explosions and a furious blaze that engulfed much of the flight deck. Sherrill was the first among a handful to die in the emergency. He was posthumously awarded the Navy-Marine Corps Medal for his heroism. AN Larry Sowers was also awarded the medal for pulling several men from the flames during an all-out effort by the crew to save personnel and extinguish the fire.

A technological first to the ship came in 1963 when the *Saratoga* was the first and only Navy ship at the time to have installed TIROS, a weather satellite system. The satel-

The Saratoga *off Brooklyn in 1956. (Courtesy of George Tanis)*

lite could photograph an area of one million square miles and then transmit the photograph to surface receiving stations around the world. The system could detect weather disturbances early and follow existing storm centers. According to command history, the first TIROS photographs came in on December 31.

The year 1964 found the *Saratoga* offshore Florida and Norfolk in qualification and training exercises. In one of the exercises, Operation Longhorn, aircraft from *Saratoga* on the East Coast and jets from the USS *Coral Sea* on the West Coast simulated air strikes on Dallas, Texas. The May 21 exercise demonstrated that carrier-based aircraft could make long-range strikes.

THE SIX-DAY WAR

Saratoga's next call into action during real-life conflict came on June 8, 1967, during the Six-Day War in the Middle East. At 2:09 p.m., nine minutes after Israeli planes attacked the U.S. intelligence ship *Liberty*, *Saratoga* was the first to hear the ship's distress calls. For the next few hours, *Saratoga's* communications station maintained a link with the *Liberty*. Both *Saratoga* and the USS *America* were on standby until the ensuing political tensions between Israel and the United States were calmed. The fighting in the Middle East kept *Saratoga* in the area, passing through the Strait of Messina three times in six days.

Joseph Stelma

Joseph Stelma enlisted in the Navy in 1962 at age seventeen. He served in V-4 Division, aviation fuels, on the Saratoga's *flight deck during three Mediterranean Sea cruises. He was aboard when the ship patrolled the coast of Cuba in December 1962 during the Soviet missile crisis.*

I went aboard her November 7, 1962, when she was in Portsmouth, Virginia, at the Norfolk Naval Shipyard dry dock. She still had the old propeller planes used in the Korean War. I was assigned to V-4 Division fuels. The next thing I know, I'm on the deck with a chipping hammer and a scraper, scraping off paint. This chief comes in and says: "We want to be able to eat off these fuel station decks any time of the day and night." I responded: "Yes, sir." My dad was a thirty-year Chief Boatswain's Mate, so I knew what a swab was.

We weren't supposed to get underway for several months. All of a sudden we're told to get things ready for sea. We're rushing. We get underway, and the skipper [Captain Frederick T. Moore] gets on the horn and announces that we'll start loading ammunition off the coast of Norfolk. I got down to the hangar bay and these large barges came alongside, and we start unloading bombs and missiles. More than our normal. Anything that was practice had a yellow ring around it. These didn't have it. These were the real thing.

We were en route to the coast of Cuba to relieve the USS *Enterprise* following the Russians' refusal to remove their missiles. We went into battle alert. Everything was general quarters. We saw the missiles coming out with the big ships leaving Havana. [The *Saratoga* spent ten days "on the line," as part of a convoy of ships.]

One night near Sardinia, we had been flying all day and were sitting around on the bunks talking. General quarters sounded. All of a sudden a guy comes over the horn: "Fire on the flight deck. All hands muster." I got on the flight deck and all I could see was fire. The whole back of the ship was ablaze. They had launched a group of planes and were spotting the deck for the next sortie. A plane landed while they were still spotting the deck. It crashed into a row of planes. When there's fire aboard ship you immediately begin helping. I was the second man on the hose. The next thing I know, we were on the wing of an A-4 Skyhawk. This thing is completely engulfed and we're standing on the wing trying to put it out. You hear explosions and rounds going off. The crane pushed a handful of planes overboard. After a few hours everything was under control.

The Saratoga *refuels the destroyer* William R. Rush. *(Courtesy of Ernie Haakenson)*

At the end of 1967, she headed back to the United States and passed through "one of the most vicious storms ever recorded in the North Atlantic." The ship was forced to reduce her speed to three knots, according to a report in *The Hook*.

Saratoga spent the next year parked in the Philadelphia Naval Shipyard undergoing a $50 million overhaul and modernization.

THE *SARATOGA* WELCOMES PRESIDENT NIXON

On May 17, 1969, President Richard Nixon made his first visit aboard the ship when he sat attentively on the flight deck, looking through binoculars to watch a firepower demonstration near the Virginia Capes for Armed Forces Day.

Between Nixon's first and second visit to the ship, the chills of the Cold War were apparent. Russian flyers were caught shadowing the ship numerous times. *Saratoga* aircraft tracked and photographed encounters with Soviet surface forces, submarines, and aircraft in the waters off Cuba, during trans-Atlantic passages and in the Mediterranean. Soviet buildup in the Mediterranean, the hijacking of a Trans World Airlines plane to Syria, and a coup in Libya drew the *Saratoga* as part of a threatening presence in the area. Another crisis in Lebanon put the ship in a "show of force"

President Richard M. Nixon and Admiral Thomas H. Moorer, Chief of Naval Operations, use binoculars to view an air and sea power demonstration from the flight deck of the Saratoga. *(Navy Photo by PH3 Philip J. Fraga)*

mode in the eastern Mediterranean.

Nixon helicoptered aboard the *Saratoga* on the twenty-eighth of September 1970, as the ship was transiting west of Naples. That evening, Nixon learned that Gamal Abdel Nasser, president of the United Arab Republic, had died. In the tenuous geo-political world of the Middle East, consequences of Nasser's death could be critical. *Saratoga* became the initial conduit to pass developing information to Nixon. Again, *Saratoga* was part of a team of carriers that subsequently maintained a show of strength, hoping to keep Middle East tensions in check.

THE *SARATOGA* IN VIETNAM

Between *Saratoga*'s eleventh and twelfth Mediterranean cruises, the ship was ordered to proceed to the Gulf of Tonkin to provide additional air power against the North Vietnamese. When orders came through on April 8, 1972, many crew members were on leave, enjoying time with their families before the next departure for the Mediterranean in three weeks. Instead, during the next sixty hours, officers and crew members were recalled from all over the country. A continuous stream of trailer trucks brought supplies for the ship. About

2.5 million pounds of supplies were loaded, and the entire air wing was assembled.

When the ship left Mayport around 8:00 p.m. on April 11, it marked the first time in its history *Saratoga* was going into combat. By May 8, *Saratoga* arrived at Subic Bay, Philippines, which would be her new "home port" during the Vietnam deployment. Operating off the coast of southern Vietnam, *Saratoga's* aircraft dropped thousands of tons of bombs in thousands of sorties as part of the effort to stem North Vietnam's invasion southward. A key part of *Saratoga's* mission was to choke off North Vietnam's supplies from heading south. Aircraft bombed enemy troop concentrations, pontoon bridges, railway crossings, supply-laden sampans on inland waterways, and barges running supplies down the coast. Typically, there were nine launches during the day and nine at night under the red lights, which meant twenty-four-hour operations. Crew members had to catch some sleep whenever they could. Meals were served twenty-three hours a day — closed one hour for clean up — to keep the crew going.

John Brandman, who was attached to a squadron from Albany, Georgia, that rushed to the *Saratoga* just before it left for Vietnam,

(Courtesy of George Tanis)

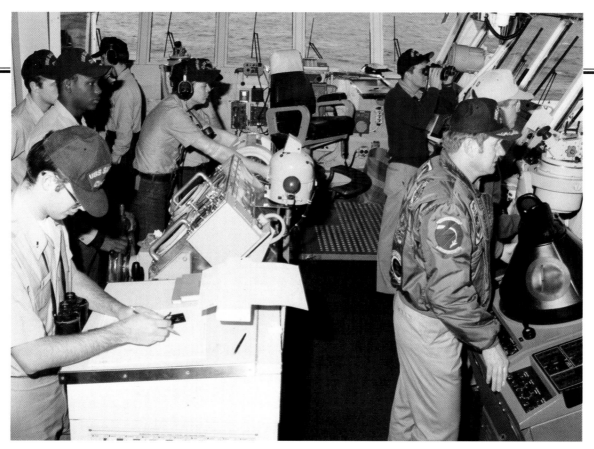

On the bridge. (Courtesy of Donald Howe)

recalls launching sorties to stop large convoys of North Vietnamese. "I remember one day we were having a stand down. The aircrew was pulling maintenance on the airplanes. At midnight an announcement came over the public address system that there was a big convoy coming down the Ho Chi Minh trail. They activated us, the *Enterprise*, the *Kitty Hawk*, and another ship. We had to get everything ready. By about 4:30 a.m. all the ships were launching airplanes to go blow up this big convoy. After we'd blow it up, slave labor over there would have it rebuilt and traffic would move again in no time. It was an endless-type situation, but we did what we set out to do."

During *Saratoga*'s combat in Vietnam, twelve aircrew members were killed or missing in action, and daring helicopter rescues of pilots downed in the water and inland were performed. On the night of August 6, a SAM missile shot down pilot Lieutenant Jim Lloyd as his A-7 Corsair was on its way to a bombing mission near Vinh. Lloyd ejected and could hear "voices of searching North Vietnamese ringing out all around him," a command history narrative reported. Two North Vietnamese found Lloyd, poked him in the back with a rifle barrel, but left him for dead. He ran, and within a half hour saw the searching helicopters. One came in close, but Lloyd missed the rescue hook. Despite enemy fire, another helicopter landed about 100 feet away, and Lloyd ran and dove in. Ground fire continued as they pulled up to safety.

Saratoga crew and aircraft were commended for providing cover for the worn-down territorial forces of Pleiku Province as they fought desperately to defend themselves against enemy fire in the village of My Thack on October 20, according to the ship's history.

During her duty in Vietnam, *Saratoga* pilots dropped more than 14,000 tons of bombs on enemy targets and flew nearly 15,000 missions. *Saratoga* left southeast Asia on January 7, 1973, and headed back to Mayport and then on to Portsmouth for an overhaul.

Saratoga would complete five more Mediterranean cruises before heading in for the most massive overhaul ever conducted on a Navy ship. At a cost of $550 million, nearly every part of the ship would be ripped out and replaced. The twenty-five-year-old *Saratoga* was to be the first among four steam-powered carriers slated for the Service Life Extension Program designed to add fifteen more active years to the thirty-year life expectancy of the ships. At the time, *Saratoga*'s assistant maintenance manager, Commander A. H. Wirzburger, remarked: "It'll be like reworking a '56 Chevy."

Two billion dollars for work on the four carriers and a minimum of 2,000 jobs over the next ten years to the shipyard awarded the contract made the stakes high. The contenders, the shipyards at Philadelphia and Newport News, Virginia, fought furiously for the contract. Political battles ensued, including open fighting on the Senate floor. In the end, the Philadelphia Naval Shipyard won.

Soon after *Saratoga* transited the Delaware River in the fall of 1980 and arrived for her long-term revamping, the crew was reduced to a mere 1,474. Building number 620 at the shipyard became her

home for the next three years. Even after the initial overhaul, problems persisted and the ship was recalled for more repairs. The Philadelphia shipyard was publicly criticized for shoddy workmanship. The ship left Philadelphia in February 1983 and was ready for her seventeenth Mediterranean cruise in the spring of the following year.

THE *ACHILLE LAURO* AND "THE LINE OF DEATH"

The eighteenth Mediterranean cruise would prove to be remarkably eventful. In early October, 1985, PLO terrorists boarded the Italian luxury liner, *Achille Lauro*, as passengers. Their plan was to get off the ship when it docked in Ashdod, Israel, and engage in terrorist attacks. But a waiter on board accidently discovered the terrorists in their cabin cleaning assault weapons. On October 7, the terrorists seized the cruise ship thirty miles west of Port Said, Egypt. They shot and killed a wheelchair-bound American, Leon Klinghoffer, and threw his body overboard. The hijackers threatened to kill others and blow up the ship if their demands weren't met. As events unfolded, the Egyptians promised the terrorists passage out of the country if they surrendered. Under darkness early the next morning, the hijackers rode a battered tugboat to shore. The hijackers and two PLO officials boarded an Egyptian Boeing 737 that took off and headed for Tunisia, a PLO outpost. But just before the Egyptian airliner took off, seven F-14 Tomcat fighter planes launched from the *Saratoga* and two E-2C Hawkeye surveillance planes tracked the airliner. The ship's historian gave the following account of the interception of the 737: "The *Saratoga*'s Tomcats loitered behind the 737, flying without lights in darkened cockpits and traveled under radio silence. The F-14s overheard the Egyptian pilot radio Tunis for permission to land. Permission denied. The pilot then tried Athens. Permission was also denied. Then, as the airliner turned to return to Egypt, the Tomcats moved in. The American fighter pilots turned on their lights and closed alongside both wings of the airliner. The F-14s dipped their wings in the international signal for a forced landing. The E-2C Hawkeye radioed the 737 to follow them. Realizing he was in a no-win situation, the pilot agreed and followed the Tomcats to Sigonella, Italy." American and Italian military surrounded the plane and the suspects were taken into Italian custody for prosecution.

Soon, *Saratoga* would be engaged in further anti-terrorist maneuvers. In early 1986, the ship began drills off the coast of Libya with the USS *Coral Sea*. *Saratoga*'s crew was informed the deployment would be extended, the planned homecoming delayed. By the end of March, the show of force would be impressive, including three carriers: USS *America* had steamed across the Atlantic Ocean to rendezvous with *Saratoga* and *Coral Sea*. *Saratoga* crew members reported that U.S. and Libyan jets had frequent encounters in the air space. The United States was resolved to defy Libyan leader

Colonel Moammar Khadafy's claim over the all waters of the Gulf of Sidra, well beyond the twelve-mile territorial limit respected by the United States.

Reports came in on March 24 that Soviet-made missiles fired at, but missed, U.S. fighter planes defying Khadafy's "line of death" about forty miles offshore in the Gulf of Sidra. The United States responded, striking four Libyan patrol boats and a Soviet-built surface-to-air missile installation near Surt. An A-7 attack jet from the *Saratoga* fired HARM missiles at the Surt battery. The next day more A-7s returned to completely wipe out the missile site. During the strikes, A-6 Intruders from *Saratoga* and *Coral Sea* destroyed patrol boats.

Airman Arthur Nye remembers raucous cheering on the flight deck when the first group of aircraft came back and the missile mounts were empty — a clear sign strikes had been made. "Everyone was screaming and yelling," Nye recalled. "We knew then we'd be on our way home."

By March 27, the U.S. ships withdrew from the Gulf of Sidra and steamed north toward Sicily to anchor for a breather. On April 16, *Saratoga* sailed into Mayport.

The nineteenth Mediterranean cruise offered quite a contrast to the engagements with the terrorist and hostile Libyans. "It turned out we found a nice little window in the world when there was stability in the Mediterranean," recalls Vice Admiral David Frost, the ship's commander at the time. But following the peaceful cruise, the ship headed in for yet another major workup. "It hurt me

A Nanachka II Soviet Missile Corvett Gunboat burns off Libya's "Line of Death" after aircraft from the Saratoga attacked the ship on March 24, 1986. The strike was in retaliation to surface-to-air missiles being fired at American planes earlier in the week. (Official U.S. Navy Photo, Courtesy of Donald Howe)

to drive that ship into the shipyard. It was working perfectly," Admiral Frost said.

Following the nineteenth Mediterranean cruise, the ship went into Norfolk Naval Shipyard for a massive $280 million, sixteen-month overhaul, which came about five years after the $550 million SLEP rebuilding. Among the new repairs and modifications, *Saratoga*'s catapults and arresting gear were upgraded to handle new F/A-18 Hornet strike fighters which would replace the aging A-7 Corsair attack jets that had long been a part of *Saratoga*'s aircraft arsenal. The ship got a new combat computer system, a new weapons elevator, modification of aviation gas tanks to hold jet fuel, and maintenance facilities for the Hornets.

Crewmen working in primary flight control wear MCU-2P protective masks during a nuclear-biological-chemical (NBC) drill aboard the Saratoga *during Operation Desert Shield. (Navy Photo by CWO2 Ed Bailey, USNR)*

SARATOGA AS SHIELD AND STORM

From the shipyard, *Saratoga* headed into an eventful deployment. During that period, the ship shuttled back and forth six times through the Suez Canal as she participated in Desert Shield and the subsequent combat operations against Iraq in Desert Storm. A grim ferry accident drowned twenty-one sailors.

Iraq's invasion of Kuwait on August 2, 1990, occurred just five days before *Saratoga* had planned to leave for a regular deployment. It was clear to the skipper, Captain Joseph Mobley, that *Saratoga* would be pulled into the troubles with Iraq. "We suspected that we would be engaged in that somehow, but no one at the time had any concept of what a big operation it was going to be," recalled Rear Admiral Mobley.

Saratoga raced at impressive speeds across the Atlantic Ocean, gulping large quantities of fuel. The old ship's swiftness surprised most everyone on board. Three weeks after the Iraqi invasion, *Saratoga* had passed through the Suez Canal to relieve the USS *Eisenhower*. As the only carrier in the Red Sea at the time, aircraft were flying day and night in an incessant grind — even more launches and recoveries than after the war commenced, Mobley said. When the USS *Kennedy* and USS *America* reached the Red Sea, *Saratoga* returned to the Mediterranean for NATO exercises for a period, and then moved back into the Red Sea.

Only one of the three ships received leave to go to the Holy Lands during the holiday season. *Saratoga* got the opportunity, but it turned out to be a bleak tragedy for the crew. A few days before Christmas 1990, a fifty-seven-foot chartered ferry, *Al-Tovia*, capsized 200 yards offshore as it pitched and rolled in swells in Haifa Bay off the coast of Israel.

One hundred and two *Saratoga* sailors and Marines were aboard, returning from shore leave. The first night two bodies were recovered. Israeli scuba divers went down the next morning and found eighteen more. One sailor remained missing and was presumed dead.

Rear Admiral Mobley was ashore and had just gone to his hotel room when the ferry capsized. "I just walked up to the window of the hotel room and looked out over the harbor and saw lights flashing and Israeli helos circling," Mobley remembered. "I thought it was a security alert. A few seconds later my

The Saratoga *passes through the Suez Canal during Operation Desert Shield. (Official U.S. Navy Photo)*

Commander Mark "MRT" Fox

During the Persian Gulf War, Mark Fox, then a lieutenant commander, was a F/A-18C Hornet pilot with the Sunliners VFA-81, part of CVW-17 attached to the USS Saratoga. He made the Navy's first Iraqi MiG kill of the Gulf War on January 17, 1991.

We launched the first strike of the war, a wave of attacking aircraft to suppress the Iraqi air defenses around Baghdad, just prior to midnight on the sixteenth.

I woke early the morning of the seventeenth after a short, sleepless night, and called the Ready Room to find out if all our aircraft had returned. I learned that Sunliner 403, flown by Lieutenant Commander Scott Speicher, was unaccounted for [Speicher was the first Allied casualty of Desert Storm]. I breathed a prayer for him, convinced myself he must have diverted or, worst case, successfully ejected, then built a mental wall against the flood of emotions crowding into my mind.

I flew in the first daylight strike launched from *Saratoga*, a complex, thirty-five plane attack against a western Iraqi airfield.

Tensions were high as we crossed the Iraqi border at about 2:00 p.m. Although there were knotted stomachs and dry mouths in anticipation of our first combat, there was also a grim determination to accomplish the mission regardless of the opposition.

As we approached the target, a warning from the E-2 to the Hornet strike element finally registered: "400, bandits on your nose, fifteen." I immediately selected a Sidewinder, got a radar lock on a head-on, supersonic Iraqi MiG-21 Fishbed and, after getting a good tone, fired it. Concentrating on the rapidly closing Fishbed, I lost sight of the Sidewinder and thought it wasn't tracking properly, so I selected a Sparrow missile and fired it. Seconds after the Sparrow left the rail, the Sidewinder hit him with a bright flash and puff of black smoke. The Sparrow hit the flaming Fishbed a few seconds later. As the burning MiG passed beneath me, I rocked up on my left wing to watch him go by. Although the rear half of the aircraft was enveloped in flame, the forward fuselage and wings were still basically intact. Forty seconds elapsed from the E-2 call to the first missile impact.

There was no time to savor the kills. Continuing onto the heavily defended airfield, I rolled in and dropped my four 2,000-pound bombs on a large hangar. As I came off target I could see a lot of dust and smoke from gun batteries around the field, a light carpet of flak bursts, and a crazy pattern of corkscrew smoke trails from hand-held SAMS. I smiled for the first time that day as I watched my bombs obliterate that hangar.

We wasted no time getting out of there.

Although I squeezed the trigger, I am well aware that literally hundreds of men had to do their jobs well for me to ever get to that point; the Sunliner maintenance team, flight deck crew, ordnancemen, E-2 guys, boiler techs, and a large cast of other unsung heroes who made it possible to fly off *Saratoga* in the first place deserve full credit for our combat success.

After forty-five days on station in support of Operation Desert Shield, the USS Kennedy *(CV-67) and its battle group are relieved by the* Saratoga *and its battle group. From left, the guided missile cruiser USS* San Jacinto *(CG-56), the aircraft carriers* John F. Kennedy *and* Saratoga, *and the guided missile cruiser USS* Biddle *(CG-34). (Official U.S. Navy Photograph)*

phone rang and they told me a ferry had sunk. I rushed down and spent the rest of the night on the landing trying to sort out what was going on."

Two days after the accident, nearly 2,000 sailors gathered in hangar bay number one for a memorial service. Twenty-one hats lined a table as memorial to the drowned shipmates. While a wreath was laid in the water, helicopters still searched for the body of the missing sailor.

"There's not a day that goes past that I don't think about that," Mobley said.

Soon, the crew was back at full speed, accelerating operations in the Red Sea as the

Hats at a memorial service aboard the Saratoga *represent the twenty-one sailors killed during the Haifa ferry accident in December 1990. (Official U.S. Navy Photo)*

A memorial service was held in the hangar bay for crew members killed in the Haifa ferry accident in December 1990. (Official U.S. Navy Photo)

buildup to war with Iraq continued. A United Nations' ultimatum spelled out a January 15 deadline for Iraq: Get out of Kuwait or be forced out. The fifteenth came and went with no response. Near midnight on the sixteenth, *Saratoga* launched the first wave of aircraft armed to fire anti-radiating missiles against targets in and around Baghdad. While the bombings were a success, one F/A-18 did not return to the ship. "People were standing around on the flight deck waiting, knowing there was one more aircraft," Mobley remembered. "I got on the

1MC (the public address system) and said, 'Apparently, we've had a combat loss.' Boy, you could just see the shoulders drop." Pilot Lieutenant Commander Scott Speicher, his plane hit by a SAM, became the first American casualty of the war.

"It turned into such a lopsided contest after that, most people who had not suffered combat losses probably were feeling pretty cocky," Mobley continued. "On *Saratoga* we never felt cocky. Every time we launched them, we were all praying they'd all come back."

The morning of the seventeenth they

Firing the close-in 20-mm weapons system (Phalanx). (Official U.S. Navy Photo)

An operations specialist mans a weapons system console. (Official U.S. Navy Photo)

launched again. Lieutenant Commander Mark "MRT" Fox and Lieutenant Nicholas "Mongo" Mongillo shot down two Iraqi MiG-21s and went on to complete a mission to bomb an Iraqi hangar site. Fox's strike marked the first Navy MiG kill of the war. That same night the ship lost two airplanes: pilots Jeff Zaun and Bob Wetzel were taken prisoner. Few could forget the broadcasts on Iraqi television where Saddam Hussein staged the coerced, glazed-eyed utterances of Allied POWs. Zaun's battered, swollen face was paraded before the international media and the twenty-eight-year-old lieutenant appeared on the cover of *Newsweek* shortly after the war started. "It was a horrible

thing seeing Jeff Zaun's face, but actually we all felt a great deal of relief," Mobley said. "He looked terrible, but at least he was alive." Zaun and Wetzel were released and, ironically, beat the ship back to the United States.

Saratoga's pilots endured long flights during Desert Storm. The aircraft carrier was based with two others, USS *Kennedy* and USS *America*, in the Red Sea, while the USS *Midway* and USS *Ranger* were positioned in the Persian Gulf. This provided a strategic advantage with warplanes coming at Iraq from two directions, but for *Saratoga* pilots it meant five to six hour flights, requiring mid-air refueling from Air Force tankers.

"We were highly dependent on tanking all the way across," said Captain Dean Hendrickson, *Saratoga* airwing commander during Desert Storm. "We worried about being stranded or running out of gas on the way home, but that didn't happen."

On board ship, Mobley understood that there was a nearly insatiable desire for information among the crew. In an effort to include the entire crew in the accomplish-

Officers conduct a press briefing during Operation Desert Shield. (Navy photo by CW02 Ed Bailey)

A RIM-7 Sea Sparrow is launched. (Official U.S. Navy Photo)

Tug boats assist the Saratoga into place at the pier after its deployment in the Persian Gulf for Operations Desert Shield and Desert Storm. (Navy Photo by PH2 James McCarter)

Family and friends of crew members board the Saratoga *as the sailors return from Operation Desert Storm on March 28, 1993. (Navy Photo by PH3 Lorrie Hughes-Smith)*

ments of the airwing — whether they were turning wrenches in the boiler room or assigned to a paperwork job — videotapes copied from aircraft mission recorders were played on the ship wide broadcast system, and pilots were interviewed on ship news broadcasts to explain firsthand what was going on. Every night Mobley held fireside chats with the entire crew on the 1MC, the public address system. He recalls that, even though he couldn't answer most of their questions about when the war would end, he seemed to be able to calm the mood just by passing on his thoughts and opinions. Crew members, many just teenagers away from home for the first time and now engaged in war, appreciated the nightly connection with the skipper.

Chief Richard Toppings, a ship journalist,

remembers Mobley's evening conversations with the crew. "He always referred to us as 'Gentlemen,'" Toppings recalls. "There were times he would shoot straight off the cuff, the way your dad would explain to you what the meaning of life was."

Every mission on an aircraft carrier is marked by highs and lows. There were signs that spirits were high during Desert Storm. Before the first combat launches, the signalmen decided to hoist the ship's huge battle ensign — an oversized flag based on tradition from the days when ships needed big flags to identify each other, but it was never flown on the modern ship. A spotlight was aimed on the gigantic flag so crews could see it while they were manning up. Pilots gave it a nod before launching. Even though it was difficult to get the battle ensign up through

The flight deck director signals a taxiing F/A-18C Hornet to stop as it moves into launch position during Operation Desert Storm. (Official U.S. Navy Photograph)

antennas and other obstacles, the crew wanted it up before every launch, Mobley recalled, chuckling. The bravado and pride indicated high spirits on the flight deck.

But there were low times, too. One day, Mobley invited the entire crew to the flight deck to watch a nearby cruiser fire Tomahawk missiles at Baghdad. The atmosphere was that of a football game. Sailors stood five rows deep, some singing a Beach Boys song revised with the lyrics "Bomb Iraq." Cameras flashed and video recorders turned as the cruiser launched the missiles. That night, CNN caught Hussein's propaganda machine in full gear when they broadcast footage of a small girl reportedly killed in the missile blast. "You couldn't help but hear the silence on the mess decks," Toppings recalled. They knew it likely was Hussein's treacherous propaganda, "but the mere thought of it was a rough thing for these

guys to deal with," Toppings said. In spite of these rough emotional experiences — high and low, the sailors learned to remain concentrated and keen, focusing on their jobs in the way an aircraft carrier demands.

By the end of March, *Saratoga* had operated nearly eight months from the Red Sea, flying 12,700 sorties and unleashing more than 4 million pounds of bombs on Iraqi targets. A large enthusiastic crowd cheered the crew when it returned to pierside in Mayport on March 28.

YUGOSLAVIA AND A TURKISH TRAGEDY

The following year, in her twenty-first Mediterranean cruise, *Saratoga* was off to another of the world's trouble spots. In the summer of 1992, she began patrols in the

Adriatic Sea in support of the United Nation's trade embargo against Yugoslavia, which, at that time, consisted only of Serbia and Montenegro. The ship also supported humanitarian aid delivery and was part of an international show of force to pressure an end to the ethnic fighting in the former republic.

At the end of September, *Saratoga* was among dozens of NATO ships involved in exercise Display Determination in the Aegean Sea. The exercise was a war game to test preparedness, coordination, and communication between the allied forces. The *Saratoga* was part of the "brown" forces, and their opponents were the "green" forces. Just before midnight on October 1, a sudden change in drill plans included simulated firing of Sea Sparrow missiles from the *Saratoga*. Crew members were roused from their sleep to man an empty missile control room. Confusion ensued. The missile control crew members were unsure whether this was a drill or a real threat. A few minutes after midnight, two missiles were launched against an ally Turkish ship three miles away. As the missiles exploded against the ally ship TCG *Muavenet* and fire spread from the bridge to two decks below, *Saratoga's* rescue helicopters and boats sped to the scene. Nineteen Turkish sailors were brought on board. Five, including the ship's commanding officer, were pronounced dead. The "walking blood bank" (composed of all *Saratoga* crew, summoned by blood-type need and the severity of the emergency) was mustered as *Saratoga's* medical department

worked feverishly to save lives — even risking their own lives in the face of a possible explosion. After the accident, *Saratoga's* senior medical officer Commander John Heil told *The Florida Times-Union*: "We treated them as our own. I've never had such empathy for a group of sailors in my life." A week and a half later, the crew donned dress white uniforms and stood in formation during an onboard memorial service for the Turkish sailors.

Morale was low. The crew felt they had been branded by the deadly mishap, and they didn't know if they would be allowed to continue the cruise. In a previously scheduled change of command, Captain James Drager was replaced by Captain Donald Weiss. Drager was among a group of *Saratoga* officers and enlisted men disciplined following the mishap. Drager's subsequent retirement was a disappointment, especially for the helicopter community, because he had been the first helicopter pilot to command an aircraft carrier and was poised to rise higher in the ranks.

Before the ship would be ready for what was to be its final deployment, it underwent $40 million in yard work, which included replacing its giant rudder. The ship was notified that its next cycle would be greatly compressed. Instead of deploying in October 1994, the ship would head out in January. What was normally a year turnaround, with sea trials and work-ups, was reduced to six months. Exercises during December included taking Marine helicopters aboard to demonstrate a new focus of integrating Marine

Families and friends of Saratoga *crew anxiously await their return to Naval Station Mayport at the end of the final cruise on June 24, 1994. (Official U.S. Navy Photo)*

landing operations with the ship. However, when the ship deployed on January 12 to the Adriatic, the Marines headed for Somalia.

By the time the ship was off the coast of Bosnia-Herzegovina, it had performed nearly flawlessly in work-ups, moral was back up, and the ship was in top working form. In a strong show of presence over a war-torn region, *Saratoga's* planes streaked over Serbian strongholds. The ship coped with heavy winter seas and overcast skies, but that didn't stop continuous flight operations. "Even in bad weather, the crews were going overland," Rear Admiral Donald Weiss remembers. "Maybe they couldn't see us, but they

could hear it and they knew we were there." The ship was involved in extensive exercises with a large number of NATO countries. They were constantly practicing coordinated efforts.

Tensions heightened on February 10, with a U.N. ultimatum to the Serbians: cease aggression or face strikes. The ship stood down that period, but poised for strikes if called upon. The Serbians backed off.

Weiss takes a lot of pride in how well the aging carrier performed. "To me, that was the highlight," he said. "Everyone was kind of worried about this old carrier creaking in here; and yet we were running four cats [catapults] and did an awful lot of alert launches in our off time. That old ship, it was there and ready to do it. Everyone seemed surprised, but they shouldn't have been. Our credentials since June were very good. We were confident that whatever had to be done could be done."

Later that February, Weiss had a heart attack on the ship and was airlifted to a hospital in Germany. Captain William Kennedy took over the Adriatic operations and, in four months, brought the ship home to Mayport for the last time.

A FINAL HOMECOMING

By 4:30 a.m. on June 24, wives and families began arriving at the pier at Mayport Naval Station to endure the final moments of their months-long vigils, waiting for husbands, sons, and fathers to come home. One by one, lawn chairs were unfolded on the pavement next to the pier. By the time the ship pulled in, about 8,000 people crowded the pierside, waving hand-painted signs and bursting with anticipation. Some, afraid the sailors wouldn't see their placards, hired planes to drag welcome-home messages across the sky.

For some, it was a bitter-sweet homecoming: it was the last for a carrier that had dutifully sailed the seas and endured wear and tear for thirty-eight years. Navy Secretary John Dalton helicoptered to the returning ship and addressed the crew: "You've been an example for the fleet by the job you've done. I'm proud of you. God bless you. God bless the *Saratoga*."

Almost immediately, stripping of the mighty old carrier began. A large number shipmates were quickly reassigned to new posts. Steady streams of personnel poured into the ship empty-handed and exited in long rows, hauling everything that wasn't welded into the superstructure. Fleets of moving vans parked next to the ship were loaded and motored off. A row of trailers was set up across from the ship as temporary offices for

The audience assembles for the decommissioning ceremony. (Courtesy of Diane Uhley)

There were few dry eyes at the decommissioning ceremony. (Courtesy of Diane Uhley)

A final salute to the Saratoga. *(Courtesy of Diane Uhley)*

the crew members who remained to close out the ship's thousands of spaces and take care of all the final details involved in bringing the thirty-eight-year voyage to a close.

The American flag is carried from the ship for the last time. (Courtesy of Diane Uhley)

From around the country, former ship-mates converged in Mayport to say good-bye to the huge ship. For many men there seemed to be a nagging personal imperative to both show respect for the powerful vessel and to reconnect with their rigorous, but memorable time at sea. Men, now retired from civilian occupations, harkened back to days decades ago when, as young impressionable teens, they boarded the carrier that would make an indelible mark on their lives. Others who remained in the Navy and went on to new assignments, came to *Saratoga's* retirement to give her a final salute.

On August 19, 1994, the eve of the decommissioning, a large group of former shipmates gathered to pay tribute to the *Saratoga*. Aged and mellowed in civilian clothes, members of

Sailors from the final cruise depart. (Courtesy of Diane Uhley)

the original crew, the plank owners, stood in on a ballroom dance floor. "Attention on deck," a man shouted in the din of the gathering. They came to attention as eighty-six-year-old retired Vice Admiral Robert Stroh, the first commanding officer of *Saratoga*, walked to the podium. A still-keen Stroh recounted the first time the ship had deep water under her keel and thanked the crew for getting the ship out of difficult situations. He thanked James Small, the ship's first chief engineer, for tackling the seemingly intractable propulsion problems. When Stroh led the group of old, and a few young, salts in chanting the Navy Hymn, few eyes remained

The Saratoga's *last commanding officer, Captain William H. Kennedy, was presented the American flag from the ship. (Courtesy of Diane Uhley)*

Phillip Klein and Captain William H. Kennedy at the cake cutting ceremony during the decommissioning festivities. (Courtesy of Diane Uhley)

dry. It would be a prelude to the emotional decommissioning the next morning.

Though it was a bright, clear day, a wistfulness pervaded the mood for many. The boatswain's pipe whistle was sobering. Thousands were seated facing the ship. Nineteen former commanding officers came to pay final respects.

"Now, after thirty-eight years and more than 60,000 men who have breathed life into this mighty warship, there is only a deafening silence," Captain Kennedy remarked from the quarterdeck on the elevator. "The catapults are secured, the arresting wires removed, the boilers cold, the bomb elevators are still, repair lockers are bare, damage control central is empty. No longer seen are the yellow shirts, the brown shirts, the blue shirts, the red shirts and the green shirts. In just a few sort minutes the boatswain's pipe will no longer sound the watch."

The commissioning pennant was lowered, symbolizing that *Saratoga* was taken out of action. The sailors who manned the rail during the ceremony proceeded one by one off the ship. Like history marching by, they progressed in a constant, steady course onto the pier. When the last sailor departed, the gigantic steel hull that had served dutifully when called upon stood cold and alone. ◾

Fireworks set to stirring music capped off the decommissioning ceremony. (Courtesy of Diane Uhley)

Airman Chuck Spias uses an MD-3A tow tractor to move a F-14A Tomcat during Operation Desert Storm. (Navy Photo by Senior Airman Chris U. Putnam)

On the Deck

Without the ability to launch and land airplanes on the flight deck of the *Saratoga*, it would just be the Love Boat, crew members like to say. Instead, it is a floating airport, a mobile offensive force, steaming from one regional hotbed to another. In short, it is a strategist's dream — an airfield you can take with you. Aircraft can be launched around the clock, carrying potent arsenals to conquer the enemy, or the ship can move into an area, its mere presence enough of a threat to ease tensions and force aggressors to back down, many times without even launching a strike.

Flight deck crewmen prepare A-7E Corsair II aircraft for flight operations. (Navy Photo by PH3 Mac M. Thurston)

Plane captains prepare an A-6 Intruder prior to launch, while a grape fuels the airplane. (Official U.S. Navy Photo)

Aircraft carriers like the *Saratoga* represent flexibility, a valuable characteristic in the uncertain political climate of today's world, where small volatile and violent conflicts spark unpredictably at various points on the globe. When the *Saratoga* moved into a region, it signaled a change in the United States' interest and intent. A carrier ups the ante, and it sends the unmistakable message that force is ready to be used to provide security or engage in offensive strikes. Unlike permanent land bases which carry a constant message, aircraft carriers like *Saratoga* quickly redefine a political stance.

The heart of the *Saratoga* is the technology that allowed the ship to launch planes from zero to 150 miles per hour in less then two seconds and then bring a landing aircraft to a halt within 300 feet — the length of a football field — once it touches the deck. While *Saratoga* was a sea-going vessel, the aircraft defined it. About 5,000 shipmates worked feverishly to put 100 men in the air.

The sailors below the flight deck — those retrieving supplies, sorting laundry, turning wrenches, lighting boilers — were integral to the mission. Each understood his role. "We are there to support the airplanes," said Harvey Hirsch, who served in the supply division in the late 1950s. "When the Lebanese crisis broke out, I remember what the captain told us. It is our responsibility to get our 110 planes in the air because they can wipe out any country in the world. If our ship gets hit after the planes are up, we've done our job. The mission will take care of itself."

Everyone who worked on or visited *Saratoga* was awed by the colorfully choreographed, synchronized flight operations. Flight deck and hangar crews wear assigned colored helmets and jerseys so everyone knows quickly who is who. As the time for flight operations nears, blue shirts and yellow shirts — plane handlers and plane-handling officers — make the last minute moves of the aircraft, making sure the first two launches

are in position, feeding into the catapults. Green-shirt catapult crews hook up and check the launching equipment. The grapes in the purple shirts lug big fuel hoses around, topping off the tanks. Red-shirted ordnance crews race between each plane, making sure the right bombs have been secured.

About forty-five minutes prior to launch, the pilots emerge. In green flight jackets bogged down with flight gear, they waddle up onto the flight deck. From high above in the bridge, skippers learn to recognize pilots by their walk — each with his own style. Some appear nonchalant, others business-

A plane captain cleans the windshield of an E-2 Hawkeye. (Official U.S. Navy Photo)

A crewman performs a preflight check on a Fighter Squadron 143 (VF-143) F-14A Tomcat. (Navy Photo by Lt. Joseph E. Higgins)

like. "After watching for a couple of weeks, I could tell you, without seeing a face, who it was by his walk, by the way he came to the flight deck and approached his airplane," former *Saratoga* skipper Rear Admiral Donald Weiss explained.

The first aircraft to takeoff and the last to return to the flight deck during a cycle of sorties are the rescue helicopters. The choppers hover near the carrier in case an accident or equipment failure drops a plane into the sea. Already in the air, the helicopters can begin rescue operations immediately.

Thirty minutes before the airplanes launch, the fairly quiet dance becomes thunderously loud: the jet engines fire up with a deafening roar. Safety checks are then performed until the moment of the launch. A white-shirted safety crew member kneels under the plane, its engine roaring at full speed, to make a final check on the catapult hook-in which is

poised with thousands of pounds of pressure, ready to burst forward. When the shooter, the catapult officer, and the pilot salute, the shooter signals a sailor on the edge of the deck (known as the "deck edge") who launches the plane with a simple press of a button. Until the button is pressed, the crew can back out of a launch, but once the deck edge activates the catapult, the plane is fired into the wind at 150 miles per hour.

Saratoga flight deck crews took enormous pride in running flight operations like a finely tuned Swiss watch. When the bell struck, the air boss wanted the first plane shot off the deck. The four catapults operated in sequence. With a deck-shaking *brrooommm*, catapult two would shoot its plane into the air, followed quickly by catapults three and four. A final roar from the jet in catapult one placed the fourth plane on its mission. With only the required air hole between the shots, four airplanes could be lifted into the air in twenty seconds. In about a minute, a new series of planes were set to fire off again. The evolution continued. Load and launch, load and launch. In six to eight minutes, twenty airplanes could be sent aloft.

It is a dangerous theatrical stage. Thick residual steam rises off the length of the catapult track, and colorful crews move with dispatch through it. The window of time between the last launch and the first landing is narrow. As soon as the last aircraft is catapulted, the young men quickly secure the catapults and are ready to recover the first plane. The ship is capable of bringing a plane down about every fifty seconds. As the pilot approaches the deck, he's given the

A flight deck crewman signals that a Strike Fighter Squadron 83 (VFA-83) F/A-18 Hornet is ready for launch. (Navy Photo by PH2 Bruce Davis)

An Attack Squadron 34 (VA-34) A-6E Intruder is guided onto a catapult. (Navy Photo by Lt. Joseph E. Higgins)

An FA-18 Hornet breaks the sound barrier. (Official U.S. Navy Photo)

A mini handler tracks positions of aircraft on the flight deck. (Official U.S. Navy Photo)

okay to land. He hits the deck with his tail-hook down and, he hopes, catches a rope cable stretched across the flight deck. When he feels the wheels hit, rather than slow down the engines, he pushes the throttle wide open just in case he didn't hook the wire. If the hook missed, he has to bolt off the flight deck and back into the air.

Soon, all the pilots are back on board, but there is no time for rest. The entire evolution starts again. This goes on for twelve to four-teen hours. In extenuating circumstances, the ship could sustain a continuous rhythm

A firefighting drill is conducted on the flight deck. (Official U.S. Navy Photo)

of take-offs and landings for two days —
even a third day, if necessary. But slowly the
wear and tear would begin to show. Burnout
would set in, and on a dangerous flight deck,
keen attention is vital. Therefore, the normal
routine for flying sorties involved twelve to
fourteen hours on and then eight off. The
ship could maintain that rhythm indefinitely.

Despite the level of activity and danger,
each player on the powerful playing field

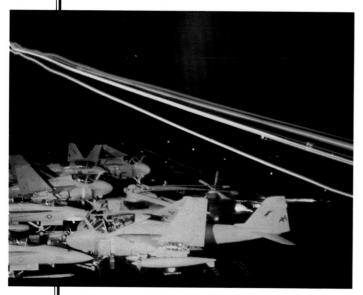

*The running lights mark the path of an aircraft
landing at night. (Navy Photo by Angelo Romano)*

seems confident and clear-headed about his
particular job and how it fits into the
sequence of events. International photograph-
er Peter Turnley, who boarded *Saratoga* three
times for *Newsweek* magazine, observed:
"You are struck that in the middle of all that
activity how seemingly professional and calm
and collected the players are. Everybody
knows what they are doing, and they do it
with an economy of gesture. Despite the fact
that life and death are very present simulta-

neously, everyone seems calm."

The dangers on a flight deck can't be over-
estimated, and *Saratoga*'s flight deck took its
share of lives. Failed launches and landings
sent aircraft over the edge. In 1963, an
errant plane landed on the wrong runway,
striking a row of aircraft awaiting launch and
sparking explosions and a flight deck fire
that killed several men. With powerful aircraft being maneuvered in a relatively small
area, jet blasts are a constant danger. Men
have been blown across the deck and sometimes over the edge, out of reach of rescue.

Flight deck crews learned to watch with a
constantly swiveling head, seemingly with
eyes in the back of their head, to duck under
passing wings, dodge the blasts, and avoid
whipping fuel lines. One young grape hauling an aviation nozzle stepped backward
into the rotating propeller of a Willy Fudd
and ripped his skin from shoulder to waist.
An airman was blown from his tractor by jet
blast and pinned against the flight deck
island, losing his right leg. There are plenty
of incidents like these to keep the level of
caution high. Even higher is the level of trust
that develops among the men who rely on
each other to do their jobs right.

"You put your life in other people's hands
all the time," said Lieutenant Commander
Dave Maynard, the officer in charge of the
catapult and arresting gear during *Saratoga*'s final deployment. "If you do something
dumb, you are going to get yelled at. It does-
n't matter what rank you are.

"When you first get up there, you are just
worried about protecting yourself. After you

AMH1 Arthur Nye

Arthur Nye joined the Navy in 1974 at age eighteen. He reported to the Saratoga *in 1978 and subsequently participated in five cruises on the ship, including the strikes on Libya and the interception of the Palestinian Liberation Organization hijackers of the* Achille Lauro. *Nye, an aviation structural mechanic, retired three months after the ship's decommissioning.*

Work starts off early in the morning, at 6:30 a.m., and you work until 6:30 at night. Out on the ship, that's seven days a week. Most of the time it's twelve hour shifts, but a lot of times we did fourteen, fifteen hour days. Working on the flight deck, you always keep your mind on the job once you get up there because it is really dangerous. I got blown down a couple of times by jet blasts. You're shaken up, but you get up and go back to work. You get bruises and just hope you don't get blown overboard next time. You've always got to look around, always keep your head on a swivel.

I was a trouble shooter. I did all the final checks on the aircraft and the catapult. You make sure everything is free and clear. You can tell. If you have to suspend a launch you just cross your arms over your head and they turn the plane around.

The biggest highlight of my career was to get my high school diploma on the ship. I had to study during my off time, staying up late in my bunk. Tutors were brought out onto the ship for classes. The Navy takes care of its own when it comes to education.

[Nye was a part of the 1986 strikes on Libyan targets.] We were on our way home, and then all of a sudden the captain announced we would be extended for a couple more months. It was six months and we're ready to get home. But the captain had kept us up to date, so we weren't surprised.

We were launching round-the-clock flights and under a lot more pressure. We were working eighteen hour days. To break up the stress, I'd try to write letters home to keep my family up to date. But you know with television, they knew more than I did sometimes. When the first strikes were made, everyone on the flight deck was happy . . . screaming and yelling. We knew then we'd be going home soon.

A plane director guides an F-14 Tomcat into position over a catapult. (Navy Photo by PH3 Mac M. Thurston)

An A-6E Intruder snags the arresting cable during landing. (Navy Photo by PH1 William Shayka)

get comfortable, then you become observant in protecting yourself and everyone around you. Everybody has to watch for everyone else; you've got blind spots you can't see."

Focus and concentration are critical, so even after grim tragedies like the December 1990 ferry accident where twenty-one sailors drowned, crew members learned quickly to put all distractions behind them and maintain absolute focus on the job at hand. That's why they were able to return to the Red Sea and launch successful sorties against Iraq.

Night operations bring new problems and more danger. Everything has to be slowed down to make successful launches and landings at night. The intervals between launches and landings are increased. For pilots, night landings on a carrier are stressful because lights are subdued, they must focus on a set of lighted wands which are the only

aid in waving them in, and they have to hit a deck that may be rocking with the current. Pilots who flew sorties over Bosnia said they weren't frightened making the flyovers, but were anxious when they thought about coming back to land on the carrier at night. "In the day time, it's good clean fun," according pilot Commander Mark Fox, who flew off the *Saratoga* during the Persian Gulf War, "But there's very little exhilaration at night. It is one of those things that requires every ounce of concentration you can muster." Day or night, launches continued regardless of the weather conditions. When *Saratoga* was engaged in flights over Bosnia, the ship had to work around bad weather during the region's winter season.

During her career, *Saratoga* used the original catapults installed when the ship was built in 1956, although some modifications were made throughout the years. The catapults

Patrick M. Broderick

As a young pilot, Lt. j.g. Patrick Broderick was attached to VA-35 Black Panthers, an AD-6 Skyraider squadron that flew off the Saratoga *from 1960 to 1963. Perhaps one of his most memorable events was a stormy pre-dawn launch February 2, 1962, about 200 miles off the coast of Sicily. A malfunctioning catapult sent his plane off the bow of the ship into the dark current.*

As I approached my aircraft across the darkened flight deck, I remember thinking that 0300 was a poor time to begin a day. I completed my pre-flight inspection as best I could in the dark, started the engine, and taxied forward to the port bow catapult. Finally, I was secured to the catapult, and it appeared this would be just another shot into the night. The cat officer dropped his wand and I braced, expecting to feel a jolt, followed by the usual acceleration.

It never came. Instead, I felt a terrifying jerk and twisting force that was throwing me over the ship's side, completely out of control. One side of the catapult bridle failed, dragging the aircraft sideways down the deck and dropping it off the end at about sixty knots. All I could do was add power, hoping that this would somehow keep me in the air.

I could see the icy white caps, followed by a terrific jolt, as the plane struck the water. I was thrown forward in the cockpit, and I felt the aircraft falling on top of me. I got out of the airplane and onto the surface. The carrier hit me and I went down one side of the hull with the waves pressing me against the ship.

I was pushing against the ship to try to get away from it but I began to feel the current drawing me under. I thought I was going to go in the screws. I thought I was dead.

The current threw me up, and I was looking right at this elevator bay . . . I could see all these sailors walking around inside. I grabbed a breath of air. The current pulled me down and I bumped around and just held my breath as long as I could. All of a sudden I popped up, looking at the rear . . . the lights of the ship. Then, it disappeared. I floated around for a while.

You can't imagine the elation I felt when, a short time later, my wingman flew overhead gunning his engine, letting me know that I had been seen and help was on its way.

A destroyer [the USS *Vesole*] found me. I couldn't move anymore by that time. A chief and two enlisted guys jumped off the destroyer in heavy water and swam over and pulled me over to the destroyer.

I thought I was in the water about a day, but it lasted about thirteen to twenty minutes.

work by harnessing steam generated by the ship's boilers. The steam is accumulated and stored, and then thousands of pounds of steam pressure is released into cylinders that force a shuttle, which is attached to the aircraft, forward into the wind. The power stroke, like a big double-barrel shotgun, shoots a plane out with steam pressure instead of gunpowder. The force is stopped, once the plane is launched, with water-brakes. A solid head of water converts the speed energy into heat.

Catapult three on the *Saratoga* was shorter than the others. The power stroke on catapults one, two, and four run 253 feet, but only 211 feet on catapult three. So, catapult three offered pilots a more thrilling ride, a harder shot. In fact, the very last airplane to shoot off *Saratoga* launched off catapult three.

Modern planes normally land on runways that stretch 5,000 to 8,000 feet. *Saratoga* could take a landing F-14 Tomcat weighing about 54,000 pounds, from 140 miles per hour (120 miles per hour relative to the flight deck) to a halt in about 300 feet. The arresting cable that stretched strong and taut across the flight deck, actually ran down the length of the ship on both sides through a winding system of pulleys to another winding assembly of cable known as the arresting engine. When the tailhook grabbed the cable, the force of motion was transferred to the cable system and stopped by pressurized hydraulic fluid.

The ship's aviation boatswain's mates (ABEs), who ran and maintained the launching and landing equipment, liked to boast that they were the hardest working people on the ship. Quite a few people who served on the ship are inclined to agree. The same sailors who launched planes and recovered them, also fixed and maintained the equipment. And the gear required an incredible amount of maintenance. "At the height of the Bosnian crisis, they were working an average of about twenty-two hours a day. They'd get two hours to take a shower, get a little nap, something to eat and then start all over again," said Lieutenant Commander Maynard, who supervised 210 ABEs. "They did that for the two months we were over there. I'd tell them to go over to the catwalk and sleep twenty to thirty minutes between launchings."

As the *Saratoga* was making its final homecoming to Mayport, former *Saratoga* shipmate Captain Mark "Spine-Ripper" Kitka flew out to the ship to be the last pilot to land and launch from the soon-to-be-retired carrier. The ship's skipper, Captain William Kennedy, served as co-pilot on the S-3 Viking to make the last arrested landing on *Saratoga*. Then Kikta climbed back into his plane, set catapult three, watched for the hand signal, and made the historic final launch off the carrier.

In all, between October 24, 1956, when a Grumman Cougar piloted by Commander William Ely made the first arrested landing, and June 23, 1994, when Kikta made the final launch, there were 363,656 catapult launches off the flight deck of the *Saratoga* and 344,664 landings. Most of the difference is accounted for by maintenance catapult shots — and a number of crashes or incidents during the Vietnam War and the Persian Gulf War when launched aircraft were shot down. ■

FA-18 Hornets pass over the Super Sara in the Mediterranean. (Official U.S. Navy Photo)

An Arsenal
of Aircraft

The program that started in the early 1950s to design and build the new series of *Forrestal*-class aircraft carriers was bolstered by the introduction of jet aircraft, fast combat planes that fulfilled the Navy's demand for a carrier-based attack combining jet power and the ability to deliver nuclear weapons. The new jets required larger fuel storage areas than the previous piston-engine planes, and the aircraft needed larger flight decks to accommodate the faster speeds.

The jet aircraft design in the works just before construction of the new aircraft carriers was the Douglas A3D Skywarrior. While the Skywarrior could operate off the flight deck of the *Midway*-class ships in action at the time, operations on the *Essex*-class aircraft carriers were deemed "marginal." So, the *Forrestal*-class of new carriers, of which the *Saratoga* was the second to be built, would serve the new jet age. The ship designs were closely aligned with the developing A3D. The hangar would be twenty-five feet high, fifty percent higher than the *Midway*-class; 750 gallons of aviation fuel

could be stored; and lifts were designed to handle the 75,000 pound aircraft, according to *Aircraft Carriers of the World, 1914 to the Present, An Illustrated Encyclopedia*.

Following *Saratoga*'s commissioning in 1956, the airplane's attached to the new super carrier "represented the most sophisticated aircraft in naval aviation inventory of the time," according to *The Hook* (Summer 1980). On board *Saratoga* were: Grumman F9F-8 Cougars, McDonnell F2H-3 Banshees, and Douglas AD-6 Skyraiders.

It was an F9F-8 Cougar — an offspring in the line of Big Cat planes Grumman began designing just before WWII — that made the first arrested landing on *Saratoga*'s flight deck on October 24, 1956. The F9F-8 was part of a series of planes with delta or swept-back wing designs. The F9F-8 was an improvement on its predecessors, touting a more powerful engine, a stretched fuselage, greater wing area [337 square feet], and larger fuel capacity [1,063 gallons]. For a time, they were standard aircraft for the Navy's carrier-based fighter squadrons. The F2H Banshee series of fighter bombers was

Inside the hangar bay, 1961.(Courtesy of Ernie Haakenson)

designed to improve on the FH-1 Phantom; it was a larger, heavier, more powerful version. The F2H-3 design gave the plane all-weather capability, greater fuel storage, an in-air refueling probe, and an ejector seat in the cockpit — the emergency escape seat was not part of all of *Saratoga*'s earliest planes.

When *Saratoga* started her first Mediterranean cruise in 1958, her formidable air squadrons included the A4D-1 Skyhawk, the A3D Skywarrior, the AD-6 Skyraider, and the F3H-2 Demon. "*Saratoga*'s first Med cruise marked the initial deployment of one of the most effective naval fighters ever developed: the Vought F8U-1 Crusader," according to *The Hook*.

Throughout the years, new aircraft and

upgraded versions were cycled onto and off of the *Saratoga*. She was the first ship to operate the A-6 Intruder, which replaced the Skyraider on Navy attack carriers in 1963. A latter version, the A6-E, with sophisticated target sensors, served as the ship's twin jet engine, low-level bomber designed to strike targets completely obscured by bad weather or the darkness of night. The two crew plane can carry five 2,000-pound general purpose bombs or a maximum of twenty-eight thousand, 500-pound bombs.

Perhaps the most controversial aircraft to join the *Saratoga* came aboard in the early 1970s, when the Navy first experimented with integrating antisubmarine warfare air operations alongside the attack squadrons.

Douglas A-1J Skyraider

(Courtesy of Ernie Haakenson)

The single-seat shipboard day attack bomber was widely used by the U.S. Navy and Marine Corps.

Wing span: 50 feet 9 inches
Length: 38 feet 10 inches
Height: 15 feet 8 inches
Weight: Empty — 12,550 pounds
   Normal loaded — 19,000 pounds
   Maximum — 25,000 pounds
Performance: Maximum speed — 318 mph at 18,500 feet
   Economy cruising — 188 mph
   Normal range — 900 miles
   Maximum range — 3,000 miles
Ceiling: 32,000 feet

Source: *The Aircraft of the World*

In 1971, antisubmarine aircraft were added to the ship to confront the mounting Soviet nuclear threat. A loud cry of resistance to the change in status came from the attack aircraft community. By necessity, adding antisubmarine aircraft required reducing the number of attack planes. However, opposition was put aside, and *Saratoga* became the test-vessel for integrating the antisubmarine warfare and the attack air wing. This was accomplished through the addition of twin reciprocating-engine, propeller-driven Grumman S-2E Trackers, dubbed Stoofs, and Sikorsky SH-3D Sea Kings before the eleventh Mediterranean cruise. After the trial cruise, opposition toward the antisubmarine component on the ship continued. The jet community felt the propeller driven S-2E Trackers were incongruent with the modern aircraft. But the introduction of a new antisubmarine warfare plane helped turn the tide. A test model of the powerful Lockheed S-3A Viking, designed to replace the S-2Es, was first flown in January 1972. Then, in June 1972, the combination of missions on the *Saratoga* was solidified when the ship's

Skyraiders line the flight deck in 1962. (Courtesy of Ernie Haakenson)

Grumman A-6 Intruder

(Navy Photo by Lt. Joseph E. Higgins)

The low-level attack bomber is designed to strike targets with a variety of ordnances in poor weather conditions or the dark of night. The Intruder, with its two-man crew, is equipped with a complex weapons system.

U.S. Navy and Marine Corps
Wing span: 53 feet
Length: 54 feet 9 inches
Height: 16 feet 2 inches
Weight: Maximum catapult takeoff weight 58,600 pounds
Performance: Cruising speed at optimum altitude, 474 mph
Accommodation: Crew of two. Bombardier/navigator slightly behind and below pilot on starboard.
Armament: Five weapon attachment points, each with a 3,000-pound capacity. Typical weapon loads are twenty-eight 500-pound bombs in clusters of six, or three 2,000-pound general purpose bombs, plus two 300-gallon drop tanks. AIM-9 Sidewinder missiles can be carried for air-to-air use. Harpoon missile capability added to weapons complement of A6E-TRAM. The HARM missile has been used on the A6-E.

Source: *Jane's All the World's Aircraft*

F-14 Tomcats (Official U.S. Navy Photo)

A Strike Fighter Squadron 81 (VFA-81) F/A-18C Hornet aircraft lands on the USS Saratoga. *(U.S. Navy Photo by Angelo Romano)*

designation was changed from CVA-60 to CV-60, the first CVA carrier to make the switch. In the latter years of the ship, the S-3B Vikings served as the Navy's newest anti-submarine warfare planes, with both surface and subsurface search equipment. The plane, carrying a crew of four, has an in-air endurance time of more than seven hours. It was used by the *Saratoga* primarily for anti-submarine operations and search missions around *Saratoga's* battle group. On August 20, 1994, at the conclusion of the decommissioning of the *Saratoga*, a group of four S-3B Vikings were part of the poignant, symbolic final flyover, thundering across the ship as thousands below looked on.

Following *Saratoga's* deployment to the Pacific during the Vietnam War, the ship went into Norfolk in 1973 for an overhaul that included equipment upgrades and the addition of jet blast deflectors to pave the way for the new Grumman F-14A Tomcat

McDonnell Douglas F/A-18 Hornet

(Navy Photo by CWO2 Ed Bailey, USNR)

The single-seat supersonic jet can operate both as a strike and fighter aircraft. The fighter and attack versions are identical, except for interchangeable external equipment.

U.S. Navy and Marine Corps
Wing span: 37 feet 6 inches
Length: 50 feet
Height: 15 feet 3.5 inches
Weight: Takeoff weight, fighter mission — 36,701 pounds; Attack mission — 51,900 pounds
Performance: Maximum speed — more than Mach 1.8.
    Maximum speed, intermediate power — more than Mach 1.0.
Accommodation: Pilot only. Two pilots in F/A-18B and F/A-18D.
Armament: Nine external weapon stations, comprising two wingtip stations for AIM-9 Sidewinder air-to-air missiles; two outboard wing stations for an assortment of air-to-air or air-to-ground weapons, including AIM-7 Sparrows, AIM-9 Sidewinders, AIM 120 AMRAAMs, AGM-84 Harpoons, and AGM-65F Maverick missiles; two inboard wing stations for external fuel tanks, air-to-ground weapons, or Brunswick TALD (tactical air-launch decoys); two nacelle fuselage stations for Sparrows or Martin Marietta AN/ASQ-173 laser spot tracker/strike camera (LST/SCAM) and Loral AN/AAS-38 FLIR pods; and a centerline fuselage station for external fuel or weapons. Air-to-ground weapons include GBU-10 and -12 laser guided bombs, Mk 82 and Mk 84 general purpose bombs, and CBU-59 cluster bombs. An M61 20mm six-barrel gun, with 570 rounds, is mounted in the nose and has a McDonnell Douglas director gunsight, with a conventional sight as a backup.

Source: *Jane's All the World's Aircraft*

fighter plane. The two-seat, multi-purpose, carrier-based fighter was developed in place of the canceled Grumman F-111B. The plane could engage up to six aircraft at one time and detect targets 115 miles away. The plane could operate in an attack mode as well, carrying up to 14,500 pounds of bombs externally. One of the features that stood out on the F-14A's flexible variable-sweep wings were small movable foreplane surfaces that could be extended forward to change the center-of-pressure position. The first operational Tomcat flew from the USS *Enterprise* in March 1974. The F-14B Tomcat that flew off of the *Saratoga* in recent years was a key weapon in long-range air-to-air intercepts and could track up to twenty-four targets simultaneously. The Tomcat could carry long-range Phoenix missiles and Sparrow and Sidewinder missiles. In 1985, a

A port bow view of the Saratoga *in November 1985. (Navy Photo by PH1 P. D. Goodrich)*

A SEAL team practices fast-roping off an H-60 Sea Hawk. (Official U.S. Navy Photo)

group of seven Tomcats and the Grumman E-2C Hawkeye, with its specialized computer and radar equipment, flew off the *Saratoga* and forced down an Egyptian 737 that carried the terrorists responsible for the hijacking of the Italian *Achille Lauro* luxury liner. The F-14 provided air cover operations during the strikes on Libya in 1986 and again in Operation Desert Storm operating out of the Red Sea.

The Grumman E-2C Hawkeye, named after James Fenimore Cooper's famous American hero, made its debut on the *Saratoga* in September 1974, replacing the E-2A/B Hawkeye with advanced radar capabilities. The plane is immediately recognized by the large circular rotating radome on its back, providing long-range early warning of enemy threats from surface vessels to fast-flying hostile aircraft. The Hawkeye also provided the *Saratoga* and fleet with air traffic control and search and rescue aid.

In 1988, following the nineteenth Mediterranean cruise, the *Saratoga* underwent a sixteen-month, $280 million overhaul which included modifications to the ship's catapults and arresting gear, and new maintenance facilities to handle the new

Grumman F-14 Tomcat

(Navy Photo by PH1 William Shayka)

The two-seat fighter plane can make long-range air-to-air strikes and maneuvers with great flexibility with its variable sweep wing. The Tomcat can track as many as twenty-four targets simultaneously.

U.S. Navy
Wing Span: Unswept — 64 feet 1.5 inches
   Swept — 38 feet 2.5 inches
   Overswept — 33 feet 3.5 inches
Length: 62 feet 8 inches
Height: 16 feet
Weight: Takeoff weight — clean 58,715 pounds
   With 4 Sparrow missiles — 59,714 pounds
   With 6 Phoenix missiles — 70,764 pounds
   Maximum — 74,349 pounds
Performance: Maximum level speed, at height — Mach 2.34
   Low level — Mach 1.2
   Maximum cruising speed — 460-633 mph
Accommodation: Pilot and naval flight officer seated in tandem.
Armament: One General Electric M61A-1 Vulcan 20 mm gun mounted in the port side of forward fuselage, with 675 rounds of ammunition. Four AIM-7 Sparrow air-to-air missiles mounted partially submerged in the underfuselage, or four AIM-54 Phoenix missiles carried on special pallets which attach to the bottom of the fuselage. Two wing pylons, one under each fixed wing section, can carry four AIM-9 Sidewinder missiles or two additional Sparrow or Phoenix missiles with two Sidewinders.

Source: *Jane's All the World's Aircraft*

Grumman E-2C Hawkeye

(Navy Photo by PH1 William Shayka)

Ship-borne all-weather early warning and control aircraft.

Wing span: 80 feet 7 inches
Length: 57 feet 6.75 inches
Height: 18 feet 3.75 inches
Maximum takeoff weight: 51,933 pounds
Accommodations: Crew of five
Maximum cruising speed: 358 mph
Endurance, maximum fuel: 6 hours 6 minutes
Mission: Can detect and assess approaching aircraft at up to 300 miles. Can track more than 2,000 targets simultaneously and automatically, and control more than forty intercepts.

Source: *Jane's All the World's Aircraft*

McDonnell Douglas F/A-18 Hornet strike fighters that would replace the aging A-7 Corsair attack jets that had long been a part of *Saratoga*'s airwing. By 1988, a series of F/A-18 C and D prototypes were developed with all-weather and night attack avionics. It takes less than an hour to switch the plane from a fighter mission to attack mode by changing external equipment. The Hornet's capabilities were demonstrated during Operation Desert Storm. Flying a F/A-18C Hornet, Lieutenant Commander Mark Fox, assisted by an E-2C, made the Navy's first MiG kill of the Persian Gulf War in January 1990, a day after the United States began its air combat against the Iraqi forces.

Among the helicopters that flew off the *Saratoga* was the Sikorsky SH-60F Sea Hawk, a gas turbine-powered helicopter that provided all-weather detection and targeting of surface ships and submarines either independently or through a data link with the *Saratoga*. The helicopter can stay aloft more than five hours. Additional missions for the helicopter included search and rescue missions, cargo transfers, medical evacuations, and communications relay.

When the *Saratoga* was ready to deploy with Carrier Air Wing, it involved mustering aircraft and equipment from beyond its Mayport base. Aircraft attached to the *Saratoga* were based at Naval Air Stations Cecil Field, Jacksonville, Norfolk, Oceana, and as far away as Whidbey Island, Washington. ◾

A Fighter Squadron 143 (VF-143) F-14A Tomcat. (Navy Photo by Lt. Joseph E. Higgins)

Agusta-Sikorsky SH-3H Sea King

An SH-3H Sea King hovers off the deck. In the foreground, the wings of an A-6 Intruder are folded to increase useable space on the flight deck. (Navy Photo by PH3 Mac M. Thurston)

Twin-engine amphibious all-weather antisubmarine helicopter. Also used for search and rescue.

Main rotor diameter: 62 feet
Length overall, rotors turning: 71 feet 10.7 inches
Height overall, rotors turning: 17 feet 2 inches
Maximum takeoff weight: 21,000 pounds
Typical cruising speed: 138 mph
Hovering ceiling: 8,200 feet
Range with standard fuel: 725 miles
Armament and Operational Equipment: Low frequency 360 degree depth sonar. Doplar radar and antisubmarine automatic equipment. Search radar, and variable speed hydraulic rescue hoist, 600-pound capacity. Two or four homing torpedoes; or four depth charges. Can be equipped with medium-range (four AS-12 air-to-surface wire guided) missiles or long-range (two Marte Mk 2 or Exocet AM-39/Harpoon) missiles.
Accommodations: Crew of four in antisubmarine role. Up to thirty-one paratroopers in troop lift role. Can be used for medical evacuations.

Source: *Jane's All the World's Aircraft*

Lockheed S-3 Viking

(Navy Photo by Lt. Joseph E. Higgins)

The Viking represents the Navy's newest carrier-borne antisubmarine warfare aircraft. A jet-powered, twin-engine aircraft, the Viking's crew can stay aloft more than seven hours.

Accommodations: Crew of four
Armaments: Four Mk 46/50 torpedoes, two nuclear depth charges, four Mk 82 560 pound bombs, or four Mk 36 destructors, all stowed internally; plus underwing armament of six Mk 82/86s, two Mk 52/55/56 mines, two Mk 60 torpedoes, two AGM-84 Harpoon anti-ship missiles, or six LAU-10C/-68A/-69A rocket pods/ SUU-44A flare pods.

Sources: USS *Saratoga* and *Jane's All the World's Aircraft*

(Navy Photo by PH1 Goodrich)

The Mission

The Navy's strategy for its aircraft carriers, such as the *Saratoga*, continued to evolve throughout the ship's career. Following World War II, attention was focused on the Pacific, but political conditions caused leaders of the United States to turn to trouble spots in the Mediterranean where the Americans maintained only limited presence. In 1946 the United States sent the battleship *Missouri* to Turkey to counter Soviet attempts to muscle partial control of the Turkish straits. Later that same year, the Navy sent the aircraft carrier *Franklin D. Roosevelt* to Greece in response to a communist-led insurgency. Soon, it was decided that a regular, consistent commitment of forces to the Mediterranean was needed. Thus began the Sixth Fleet, which became a standard presence supporting western claims to Trieste and showing the United States flag offshore troubled France and Italy. A U.S. aircraft carrier would be permanently assigned to the Mediterranean by the late 1940s. By the early 1950s, when construction of the *Saratoga* began, the mounting Soviet threat

The replinishment oiler USS Kalamazoo *(AOR-6) conducts an underway replinishment of the* Saratoga *in the Atlantic in June 1993. (Navy Photo by PHAN Werling)*

prompted the United States to increase its forces committed to the region, and in 1953 plans to build bases in Spain for the Navy and Air Force were solidified. By the time the *Saratoga* was commissioned in April 1956, the ship would be assigned to the Sixth Fleet and serve on a series of deployments in the Mediterranean to show the

A crewman signals to an auxiliary ship. (Official U.S. Navy Photo)

flag and stem conflicts in Europe and the Middle East. By the time the ship was decommissioned in 1994, she went on twenty-two Mediterranean cruises in addition to other operations.

During the 1970s, the *Saratoga* became the first Navy aircraft carrier to assume the "triple-threat" multi-mission. The concept was first tried aboard the *Saratoga* during its Mediterranean cruise in 1971. In addition to the aircraft's role in striking targets on land or sea and their defensive role of finding and destroying enemy aircraft, the ship was equipped with aircraft and technology to detect and strike enemy submarines. After the triple-threat was successfully employed

on the *Saratoga*, it eventually became a standard for all carriers.

The Sixth Fleet consists of a number of battle groups centered around the aircraft carriers. During *Saratoga*'s tenure in the Mediterranean, the number of Navy ships in the region was expanded and contracted in relation to the political conditions. Generally, conflict and combat situations resulted in forces other than the normal battle groups. Ship configurations were based on what was needed, emphasizing the flexibility of the aircraft carrier and other Navy vessels. During Operation Desert Storm, carriers were stationed both east and west of Iraq in the Persian Gulf and Red Sea to provide strikes from both directions.

Near the end of *Saratoga*'s thirty-eight years at sea, the Navy made a fundamental shift in its strategy for deploying its forces. Military downsizing and budget cuts, along with a dramatically revised post–Cold War view of the world political landscape, prompted new strategies for Navy ships. Configurations of large individual carrier battle groups moving independently were not appropriate for the new political climate. Instead of preparing only for large global operations, the Navy is prepared to respond to hotspots of conflict in several regions around the world. Part of the Navy's new mission is to quickly shuttle Marines and equipment onshore in hostile territory.

The newest structure of the forces put the *Saratoga* at the center of a fifteen ship, 12,000 person Joint Task Group that combined the carrier battle group and amphibious landing operations. The carrier's aircraft conducted command, control, and surveillance operations, along with the potential to strike targets in the skies, the seas, or on land. Anti-air protection was provided by the *Aegis* guided-missile cruisers, the USS *Philippine Sea* (CG-58) and the USS *Vicksburg* (CG-69). Hundreds of potential targets are tracked simultaneously by the advanced radar systems of the guided-missiles cruisers, supported by two SH-60B Sea Hawk helicopters. Two destroyers, the USS *Arthur W. Radford* (DD-968) and USS *Comte de Grasse* (DD-974), provide antisubmarine warfare and strike capability

with Tomahawk missile systems. Also supporting the joint task group were two *Oliver Hazard Perry*–class guided-missile frigates, the USS *Taylor* (FFG-50) and the USS *Carr* (FFG-52), providing anti-air and anti-surface warfare. In a hallmark of the new strategy, operations to land Marines for assault on shore are included. The Joint Task Group Amphibious Force included the USS *Inchon* (LPH-12) at the center of the landing force; the USS *Trenton* (LPD-14); the USS *Portland* (LSD-37); and the USS *Spartanburg County* (LST-1192). Two Los Angeles–class submarines, the USS *Cincinnati* (SSN-693) and the USS *Boston* (SSN-703), support the force with fast attack of enemy submarines or surface ships. Fleet oiler USS *Monongahela* (AO(J)-178) and ammunition ship USS *Mount Baker* (AE-34) were attached to the joint task group to supply underway replenishment of fuels and weapons. ◾

A Helicopter Combat Support Squadron 4 (HC-4) CH-53E Super Stallion idles on the flight deck during Operation Desert Storm. (Navy Photo by PH3 Terry Simmons)

A search and rescue swimmer is lowered into the water. (Official U.S. Navy Photo)

Life at Sea

A sea-going outpost. A mobile island populated by thousands.

Saratoga was designed as a nearly self-contained environment, able to survive for months at a time in its insulated world at sea. The ship approaches a high level of self-sufficiency, except for regular underway deliveries of fresh food and fuel. This nearly sequestered community touts its own hospital, stores, bank, newspaper, broadcast studio, chapel, print shop, repair facilities, high school, and college programs — even a judicial system and jail. With its full complement, when it is joined by all its aircraft, about 5,000 personnel reside in this floating city.

Each sailor who steps on board must learn to cope with navigating tight spaces; hearing repetitive, jarring noises that rise in volume during up-tempo operations; working tedious, long, grinding hours; having little, if any, personal privacy; and enduring long absences from spouses and families. During the ship's final deployment, for example, 100 sailors became fathers in absentia. The work is unrelenting, physically demanding, and dangerous. On the flight deck, one stupid mistake can kill. Loss of life was always a threat on the *Saratoga* as a result of accidents, emergencies, or combat. Each cruise book, printed at the end of a deployment, saves the next to the last page for a memorial to *Saratoga* sailors who died during that period at sea. Few cruise books could tout they brought *everyone* home.

When new shipmates first approach the massive vessel, the prospect of living on the giant ship for months on end is unsettling and daunting. For thirty-eight years, young men watched the shoreline recede as the ship pushed away from the pier. Some loved life at sea; others merely tolerated it; none went unaffected. All retain vivid memories of life at sea on *Saratoga*.

THE DAY BEGINS

0600. The high-pitched whistle of the boatswain's pipe breaks the air. "Reveille. Reveille. All hands heave out and trice up. The smoking lamp is lighted. All authorized spaces now reveille."

A petty officer shows his son the anchor during the Tiger Cruise on the final homecoming. (Official U.S. Navy Photo)

For sailors not already up and working, that means climbing out of a tight bunk, stacked three high in dormitory-like compartments that may berth as many as 198 shipmates. Home is the space between your rack and the rack above you. With little space between bunks, there's no room to sit up. The mattress and bed board lift up, coffin-like, exposing a compartment for storing personal items underneath. With bunk storage and locker, usually there's still not enough room, so sailors who are lucky grab a little space elsewhere. Privacy in the berthing spaces means sliding a thin blue

Chief Richard Toppings

Richard Toppings first reported to the Saratoga *in 1973. As part of the public affairs team, he was on the ship keeping information flowing to his shipmates during the tragic ferry accident in Haifa, Israel, the Persian Gulf War, and during the Turkish missile accident.*

When I reported to *Saratoga* back in 1973, she was sitting in the dry docks — it turned out to be a fourteen-month dry dock period in Portsmouth, Virginia. When I walked up and saw this huge ship sitting in the dry dock, I just kind of set my bag down for a minute and said, "Oh my god, I'm going to be on a ship." It just hit me: I'm going on a ship. I wound up having to do a whole lot of growing up, maturing, and adapting. Being in the yards made it rougher. The ship didn't operate like it normally did. You didn't have that teamwork. Everything is out of place while it's being worked on.

I made friends with three guys I reported to the ship with, and we went through indoctrination together. We started running around together. Then, about a month later, I just didn't see them anymore. I started wondering, why aren't they coming around? I checked down at their division and they had gone on unauthorized absence. Then, after a while, they became deserters, and I never heard from them again.

I suddenly realized that I probably was also at a make-it-or-break-it point. I just had to say: "I committed to do this. I'm going to do it."

I ended up going back for a second tour. I made chief on the ship and went through my initiation on the ship.

[*Late in the night of January 16, 1990, Toppings and his shipmates learned they would engage in war with Iraq.*] When Captain Mobley came on the intercom close to midnight and made the announcement, some guys were on the mess deck eating midrats [*midnight rations*]. I remember noticing two things: One was a lot of cheering, like at a football stadium. At the same time, you saw a lot of other people who just stopped eating and got sad. It was just that kind of mixed emotion: Oh, gosh, we're going to war. We're going to war, but at least that means it will end soon.

Shoe repair performed on board. (Courtesy of George Tanis)

Members of the flight deck crew catch a moment of rest on a cargo net. (Official U.S. Navy Photo)

curtain along a rail to shut yourself in and, hopefully, your shipmates out. Each has a small fluorescent light for reading. Bunks are personalized with photos of a sailor's wife, his girlfriend, a pet, or a beloved truck taped on the wall — reminders of what awaits back home.

The rack might not look too comfortable to an outsider, but after long hours of physically demanding work, a dog-tired sailor sleeps just fine. Except, probably, for sailors who bunk on the 03 level, just beneath the flight deck. Those so lucky can recite perfectly the sounds of a landing aircraft: the

gun-firing pop when the plane first smacks the deck, the screeching of the arresting cable, the thrust of the plane going full throttle in case it missed the wire, the engine dying down, the cable thwapping repeatedly as it hits against the deck as it is rewound. In a cycle of night flights, sailors bunking directly below the deck hear it over and over. Miraculously, most eventually learn to sleep through takeoffs and landings, though they also have to overcome a nagging fear that occasionally surfaces while they are serenaded by flight operations: What if one of those planes crashes on the deck right above me

Engine men light off one of the eight boilers on the ship. (Official U.S. Navy Photo)

with only a relatively thin layer of metal between us?

Even if a sailor isn't just below the flight deck, there are no quiet places on an aircraft carrier. Noise and vibrations of some sort are ever present — vents whooshing air, giant washing machines gyrating. When shipmates first depart the ship, many can't sleep because of the stillness, the silence. Lieutenant John Wallach, *Saratoga's* public affairs officer during the last deployment, had to keep a fan running near his bed when he first got home to prevent the peaceful

quiet from keeping him awake. Officers' berthing is a little more spacious than the enlisted men, but far from plush. Officers don't escape the ship's racket either. The commanding officer and senior offices have one-man staterooms. Other officers bunk two, three, or four to a compartment. Junior officers are grouped eight or ten in JO Jungles.

Showering on a ship takes on new meaning. Evaporators process salt water into fresh water. With fresh water at a premium, showering means pushing a button on a nozzle to release just enough water to get wet, standing in the cold and soaping up, then releasing just enough water to rinse off. If there's a problem with the water conversion system, machinery gets first dibs on fresh water. There were a number of times during the ship's history that the crew had to take itchy salt-water showers.

WORKING ON BOARD

There's no such thing as a nine-to-five job on a ship. If machinery needs repairing, crew members work until it is fixed — even if that means three days or more without a break. When round-the-clock sorties were flying, the aviation boatswain's mates who worked with the launching and landing gear sometimes worked twenty-two-hour days, as they did for a month on end during flights over Bosnia-Herzegovina on the last deployment. If the ship goes on general quarters, high-alert status, sailors stayed at their battle stations indefinitely. Duty watch meant staying on the job all night. Storekeepers, for example, rested in hammocks in the supply rooms while they were on alert in case a machinery

A machinist mate makes his mark on the control board. (Official U.S. Navy Photo)

Engineering control room in machinery room No. 3 (Official U.S. Navy Photo)

part or other material was needed. Sailors caught catnaps when and where they could, resting on a airplane wing, reclining on a cargo net.

Many jobs were hot, demanding, and dirty. Seven levels down, Brad Senter, a machinist mate in the late 1960s, worked the throttles and later supervised others in the engine room. "It was about 120 degrees most of the time," he said. "When we'd go to Cuba, it would be 130 to 135 degrees." In the belly of the ship, the only way the engine crews knew they were on a moving vessel was to watch the shafts turning. To cope with the heat, the machinists took off their shirts and sat underneath the hot air blowers, or took coffee breaks in the air-conditioned control room. Perhaps the dirtiest job was in the ship's bilge, the very foundation of the massive vessel. Senter and others had to wade knee deep in the oil and water to repair the pumps.

As difficult and complicated as it is to run an aircraft carrier, it's even more impressive when you consider the average age of the crew on *Saratoga* was a little over nineteen years. In early years, it was probably slightly younger, with sailors only seventeen years old regularly coming aboard. Teenagers, many just out of high school, ultimately, were responsible for the general success of the ship and the safety of the pilots. "Look at what eighteen- and nineteen-year-olds are doing in Jacksonville, Atlanta, Los Angeles, New York, and Chicago, and then come out and see what the eighteen- and nineteen-year-olds are achieving on an aircraft carrier," said Rear Admiral Donald Weiss, former commanding officer. "The *Saratoga* is not the officers, it's not the commanding officer, it's the team. Those eighteen- and nineteen-year-olds are a major part of the team."

Former *Saratoga* sailors have vivid memories of long chow lines, sometimes waiting forty-five minutes to an hour just to eat. Everyday, 5,000 hungry men had to be fed.

A mess specialist prepares a daily meal. (Official U.S. Navy Photo)

The crew makes its way through the chow line. (Official U.S. Navy Photo)

That added up to 20,000 daily meals prepared on board: the three standard meals and midnight rations. Carrier Onboard Delivery (COD) planes regularly brought fresh fruits and vegetables, milk, and other supplies. When the ship was built, the *Saratoga* had enough storage to stock provisions to last up to three months without resupplying, but morale would have suffered sorely without the regular underway deliveries of fresh items.

While somewhat sequestered, the ship was never cut off from the outside world. A con-stant flow of information shuttled onto and off of the *Saratoga*. As technology advanced, so too did the ability to retrieve news from the outside world. When the *New York Times* began producing a satellite-transmitted seven-page summary of its contents for cruise liners, the Navy started subscribing, too. The Times Fax was downloaded and reprinted daily. The sailors got a steady diet of news through the Associated Press wire service, which was transmitted to the ship and used in a daily newspaper, *The Ship's Log*, produced using the print shop onboard.

Onloading fresh produce on the flight deck. (Official U.S. Navy Photo)

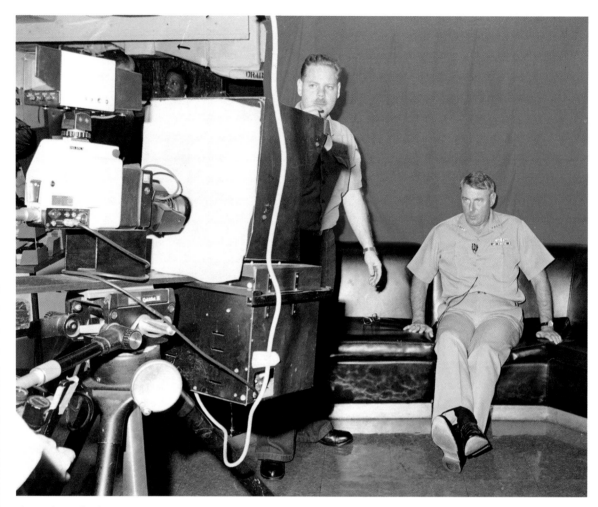

An onboard television production interview of an admiral. (Official U.S. Navy Photo)

An important lifeline was CNN International, broadcast continually in later years on one of the three television stations on the ship. Sometimes, CNN was the first place sailors would learn of world events involving their own ship. The television connection to the world outside the ship was important for morale. If the broadcast system broke, fixing it often became a top priority. With its own broadcast studio, the public affairs office produced its own informational and educational programming. During the Persian Gulf War, interviews with pilots just back from sorties were used to keep the ship informed. Sailors also looked forward to watching some of their favorite movies. The ship's video tape library had about 700 titles that could be broadcast throughout the ship.

For shipmates, shopping in the ship stores generally meant strolling to walk-up windows, and pointing to items such as soft drinks and candy bars. Though one shop, fondly called *Sara* Mall, had a few shelves and enough room to walk down the aisles.

The sixty-four-bed hospital could handle any medical problem in its initial stages and

Father Thomas Moore

Father Thomas Moore has a number of strong connections to the Saratoga. *His father, Captain Frederick T. Moore, was skipper of the ship from November 1962 through September 1963. Father Moore was a Navy pilot assigned to flight instruction in Pensacola, Florida, then later, as a Navy chaplain, he served on the aircraft carrier from June 1984 to June 1986.*

When I was a young seventeen-year-old, I went to visit the ship at Mayport when my father was taking command. The Catholic priest on board said: "One day you will be chaplain on this ship."

When I went to the ship as chaplain that first day outside of Naples, I was impressed standing on the flight deck in the open sea, even though I had a number of carrier landings myself. Having been raised in the Navy and having experienced a lot as a line officer, I wasn't intimidated. I was ready for anything that happened. In the Navy you learn to get right in there and get to work. Everything is OJT [on-the-job training] in the Navy.

Each Sunday, I had up to eight Masses. I had Mass three times on Sunday on the *Saratoga* and then would go to four different ships in the battle group. I'd go from ship to ship to ship. We also had Mass every day.

My biggest ministry on the *Saratoga* was counseling. I would counsel ten sailors a day with their personal problems, wife problems, being-in-trouble problems. Problems that every teenager has, sailors have. But sailors have them to a greater degree because they are out of their environment when they are on a ship. On a ship at sea, your problem with a wife or a family member is exaggerated a hundred times. So, it was very heavy counseling.

One of the most memorable experiences was during the *Achille Lauro* hijacker recovery. I was having Mass on board and the announcement went out to general quarters right during Mass. I had 500 guys there, and here I am right in the middle of Mass — right at the consecration. I was just going to pronounce the words, and then: "General quarters, General quarters. This is not a drill." And everybody leaves, and I'm standing there by myself. I thought, oh my goodness. They were launching to intercept the *Achille Lauro* hijackers.

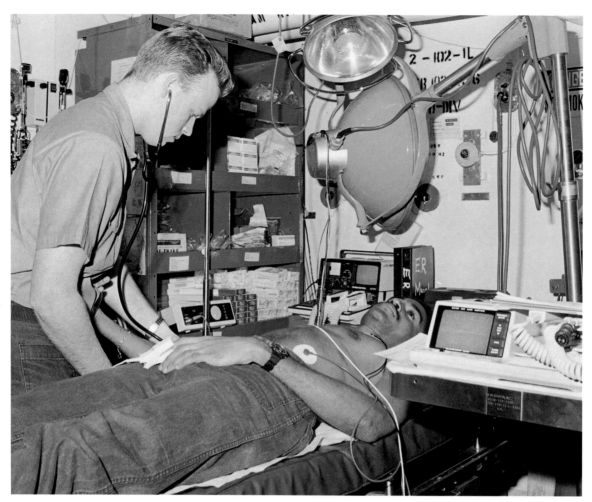

A sailor is examined in the ship's emergency room. (Official U.S. Navy Photo)

could even provide short-term stays in an Intensive Care Unit. Those requiring long-term care were airlifted off. On board, dental offices and pharmacies were also present. For spiritual or counseling needs, the ship's chaplains held religious services regularly and usually had a steady stream of sailors lined up for individual consultation. Whatever personal problems people had to deal with — especially those of young adults — were magnified tenfold on a ship. There was nowhere to run from problems, no calling in sick and staying home with your wife and

family if there was trouble with a supervisor. And any personal problems with families thousands of miles away were difficult to work out long distance.

Families got a chance to board the ship on special days for dependents. As a cost-savings measure, after a long dry dock period, hundreds of family members, pets, and cars were loaded on board to make the overnight transit from Philadelphia to Mayport. After the more than two-year massive overhaul started in 1980, more than 1,000 spouses and family members, 750 cars and trucks, twenty dogs and cats, and a parakeet traveled on the ship.

Since the ship carried thousands of men, a certain degree of anonymity pervaded. Decades after serving on the ship at the same time, shipmates met and realized they likely crossed paths on the ship many times, yet remained strangers throughout the deployment. When *Saratoga* pilot Lieutenant Commander Scott Speicher became the first Allied casualty of the Persian Gulf War, most of the crew had never met him. Some only recalled passing him in a corridor.

The Catholic Chapel on board the Saratoga *in 1960. (Courtesy of Patricia Mehle)*

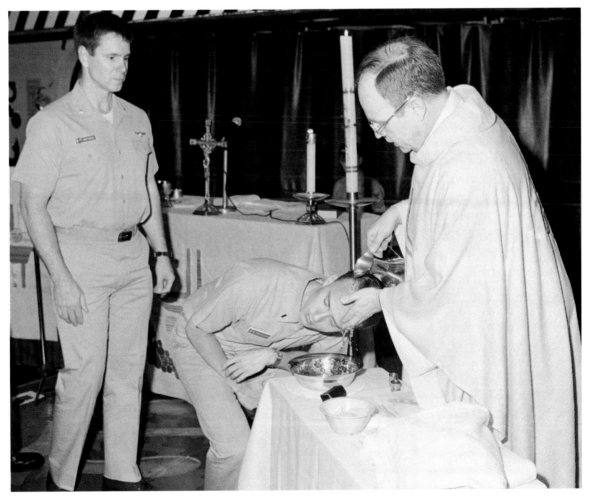

A baptism is performed during an onboard Mass. (Official U.S. Navy Photo)

A crewman browses among the available items in the ship's store. (Official U.S. Navy Photo)

WHEN FREE TIME COULD BE FOUND

Time to oneself was at a minimum on the *Saratoga*, but in between long work hours the crew had many ways to entertain and better themselves. Sailors were encouraged to complete their high school diplomas on the ship and could take college credit courses. Teachers were flown onboard to prepare students for the G.E.D. exams. Graduation ceremonies with more than a hundred men were sometimes held in the hangar bay.

"The biggest highlight of my career was to get my diploma," said airman Arthur Nye, who studied in his bunk at night and received his high school diploma during a deployment in the mid-1980s. Colleges from around the country sponsored educational programs. Even when the *Saratoga* participated in the Vietnam War, four professors from Jacksonville University met the ship in the Philippines. According to the ship's historian, 208 sailors enrolled in seven different college credit courses offered.

Shipmates could work off steam in the small weight rooms crammed with equipment. But sometimes that meant waiting in line for a chance to work out. With space at a premium on the ship, exercise gear such as life cycles was set up in passageways. Finding a place to jog or run was a challenge. "You can run on the ship if you can find room in the hangar bay," Lieutenant John Wallach recalled. "It's more of an obstacle run, though. You have to duck under wings and horizontal stabilizers, jump over tie down chains and watch out for aircraft being respotted and ground equipment driving around."

Basketball teams competed on courts in the hangar bay and sports teams, such as softball, tennis, and soccer, competed with teams from other ships in the fleet or organized games with teams in port cities. Indoor boxing smokers were organized, complete with champion trophies. Sailors remember swim calls, when the ship stopped to allow crew members to dive into the deep sea. Russ Doerr, one of the original crew members, remembers a swim call near Guantánamo Bay in the late 1950s. Sailors dove off elevator Number 3 into the Caribbean Sea. "They'd put motor whaleboats out on the perimeter with Marines holding rifles in case any sharks would come," Doerr recalls. Crew members organized bands, with rock concerts (obviously in the later years) held in the hangar bay.

Sailors sometimes were airlifted off during a deployment because of a personal crisis.

The American Red Cross played a big role in relaying messages to and from the ship regarding sailors' personal matters. During the last deployment, for example, when a sailor's father had a heart attack in Houston, the doctor got in touch with the local Red Cross, which in turn notified the ship. The same day the ship received the doctor's message, the crew member was flown out to see his dad. The Red Cross also sent birth

A basketball tournament is held in the hangar bay. (Official U.S. Navy Photo)

Boxing matches were held in the hangar bay as entertainment for the men. (Courtesy of George Tanis)

announcements to the ship. During the final Mediterranean cruise, 100 sailors became new fathers.

There were 2,300 telephones on board for communications among the thousands of compartments, and in recent years a satellite telephone link allowed crew members to call home for six dollars a minute. Newer carriers now have a constant satellite link and pay phone boxes where sailors can drop in coins, at fifty cents a minute. The COD brought coveted daily mail and packages.

Though the ship was large, it was difficult to find a place for solitude. In a personal daily diary chronicling his Navy career, including boarding the *Saratoga* at age twenty-one, Quartermaster John Yovanovitch wrote in an October 10, 1961, entry:

Recently I have discovered a place on the ship where I can get away from everybody. The place is Secondary Conning Station, which is located way up in the bow of the ship. There I read, write letters, and study. Tonight and a few nights ago, I saw a couple of beautiful sunsets. Both times we were heading West and the sun was in full view. In front of us, some 3,000 yards away, was the outline of our destroyer escort.

Throughout the years, the ship hosted hundreds of visitors both in port and while underway. Kings, queens, presidents, and dignitaries toured the ship at foreign ports; popular entertainers were flown on board to boost morale, including everyone from Bob Hope to the Dallas Cowboy cheerleaders.

Port visits meant periodic rejuvenation from the tough ship life. For many men, it was a chance to experience foreign cultures and see famous sites from around the world — opportunities they likely wouldn't have otherwise had. *Saratoga* sailors toured many countries, including Italy, Spain, Greece, Sicily, France, Scotland, England, Israel, and Hong Kong. Typically, the crew rotated duty, leaving a third of the shipmates on board each day at port. Machinist mate Senter recalled one unforgettable port visit: "I got to dance with Sophia Loren at the Cannes film festival in 1962." He'd heard about one of the parties associated with the French film festival. He and some buddies bought civilian clothes and joined in. Yovanovitch filed this entry in his diary on January 25, 1962:

We left Venice, that beautiful city built on water. We stayed in the luxurious Hotel Luna. We toured the city both by foot and gondola. Its beauties are enormous and one cannot see everything in three days. So, my dream of seeing Grande Canal, gondolas, Porto Rialto and Piaza di S. Marko came true. The tour ended at midnight by our return to the ship.

After a few hours' sleep, Yovanovitch went onto Pisa and climbed the Leaning Tower in the morning and visited Florence in the afternoon.

These port visits were a chance for sailors to see the world and let off some steam after long periods of hard work and being cooped up on the ship. Certainly, sailors got into their share of mischief and trouble during

Bob Hope and Miss World entertain the crew during a Christmas show at Gaeta, Italy, on December 22, 1969. (U.S. Naval Historical Center Photograph)

port visits. As one officer explained: "Everything you've heard about sailors in port is true. They love going into foreign ports and having a good time, that is all part of it."

Port cities around the world became accustomed to the *Saratoga*'s lights at night. The lights strung from the carrier's bow to stern, illuminating the ship at night, were sometimes called the Mediterranean Lights. Regular port cities counted on the protection

Whitney Houston was one of the many celebrities to visit the ship and entertain the crew during long deployments. (Official U.S. Navy Photo)

and relationship those lights portrayed.

While the beauty of some of the port regions impressed the sailors, they also were discomforted by the abject poverty they witnessed in some foreign ports. Many engaged in charity work for needy locals. For example, starting in the 1960s, the ship adopted an orphanage in a slum of Naples and invited children onboard for Thanksgiving and

Christmas holidays. The officers wives' collected clothing and other necessities for the orphans. In France, sailors aided the small town of Frejus in 1959 after 200 residents died when a dam burst and flooded the town near Cannes. During the Vietnam deployment, the crew raised money to support relief efforts in the flood-ravaged central Luzon provinces. Also, after bringing forty

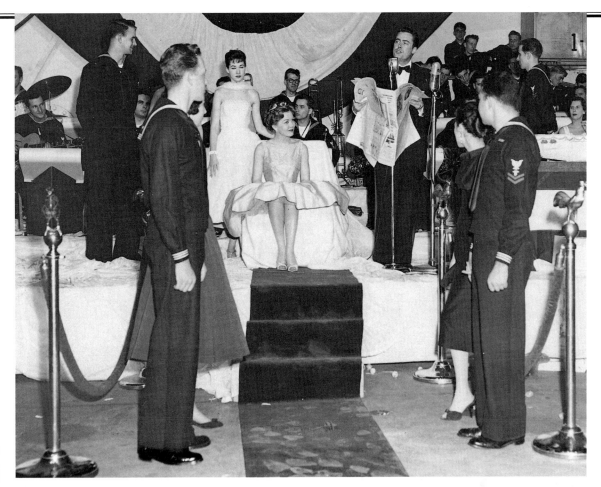

Beauty pageants and bands were special entertainment for the sailors in the '50s. (Courtesy of George Tanis)

Thanksgiving dinner is served by Saratoga *sailors to orphans in Naples, Italy. Also serving are (from left) Marcia Grosvenor, Mrs. McDonald, and Patricia Mehle. (Courtesy of Patricia Mehle)*

Filipino orphans aboard for Christmas gifts and festivities, the ship raised $25,000 in five days for badly needed repairs at the orphanage just a few miles from the naval base in Subic Bay. During the final deployment, seventy-five sailors visited a refugee camp in Slovenia. They painted the camp dormitories, played sports with the children, and the ship's twenty-seven-piece band played for the refugees. ■

The USS Saratoga *(CV-3) circa 1933, forerunner to the CV-60. (U.S. Naval Historical Center Photograph)*

The Saratoga Legacy

The legacy of U.S. Navy fighting ships bearing the name *Saratoga* began on a 2,800-acre battlefield in Saratoga County, New York, where an overwhelmed and exhausted British force surrendered to American forces, turning the tide of the Revolutionary War. On September 19, 1777, the Royal army and a contingent of German troops advanced in three columns on an American camp just southeast of Saratoga Springs. The British won the initial skirmishes, but not without suffering heavy losses of men and supplies. The British entrenched themselves for three weeks waiting for fresh support. It did not arrive. In the meantime, the American forces expanded. Holed up, with little hope of additional men being sent as support, the British faced a dilemma: retreat or advance. On October 7 they advanced, only to face severe losses in the first hour of battle. Over three weeks of fighting, the British had suffered 1,000 casualties compared with 500 American dead. The British retreated north, trudging through mud and rain. Reaching high ground, they took refuge in a fortified camp.

American forces that had grown to 20,000 surrounded a weary Royal army. The British surrendered on October 17, 1777, and marched out of the encampment and stacked their weapons on the west bank of the Hudson River. The victory ended British attempts to split the American colonies into two unconnected bases, and inspired France to join the war as an American ally. Thus, the battle was an important advance in the American fight for independence.

About two-and-a-half years later, the first Navy ship to bear the name *Saratoga*, in honor of the battle, was launched in Philadelphia. An eighteen-gun sloop-of-war, the *Saratoga* transported military supplies and captured a number of British ships. In 1781, *Saratoga* separated from a convoy of ships to pursue two fleeing enemy ships. After the first was captured and an American crew put in place, the *Saratoga* gave chase to the second ship. Suddenly, the winds became ferocious. Crew members on the captured ship watched as the *Saratoga* disappeared. The ship was never heard from again.

Saratoga Springs, New York

The USS *Saratoga* had strong community relationships beyond its home port in Mayport, Florida. As the site of the Revolutionary battle for which all six Navy *Saratogas* were named, the city of Saratoga Springs and surrounding Saratoga County in New York have long felt a bond with the series of Navy ships named *Saratoga*. The city and county have an active patronage to their namesakes.

Saratoga Springs was involved with the USS *Saratoga* (CV-60) from its inception to its decommissioning. City representatives visited the New York Naval Shipyard at Brooklyn in 1952 as the aircraft carrier's keel was laid. They came back at the christening to honor the nearly completed ship and took a prominent role in the ship's commissioning on April 14, 1956.

Soon after the commissioning pennant was hoisted, Saratoga Springs Mayor Addison Mallery presented the ship with an elaborate silver service as a symbol of the residents' affinity with the powerful new aircraft carrier.

The custom-crafted Gorham epergne had been purchased with funds raised in Saratoga County, and it was presented to the fifth USS *Saratoga* (CV-3) thirty-three years earlier. The silver service was removed from the heroic World War II ship before it was sunk in an atomic bomb test in 1946.

The silver service is only a symbol of the larger support the city and county gave the latest aircraft carrier throughout its thirty-eight-year career. Saratoga Springs hosted large groups of visiting sailors, and, in troubled times, rallied to raise funds to support the sailors and their families at home. For example, during Desert Shield and Desert Storm, residents of Saratoga County gave more than $100,000 in donations. A planeload of gifts, cookies, and ice cream was sent to the sailors' children, while a cargo of video games, musical instruments, and 60,000 bingo cards requested by the ship was sent across the sea.

After the decommissioning, the silver service was brought back to New York where it will be placed in the Saratoga National Historical Park, at the site of the namesake Revolutionary War battle that turned the tide in the war.

Larry Gordon, a liaison between Saratoga Springs and the ship, hopes one day there will be another *Saratoga* ship to receive the service. "We are ready to give it back tomorrow for another ship named *Saratoga*."

The second *Saratoga*, a twenty-six-gun corvette, was christened the same day Napoleon abdicated, April 11, 1814, and served as a flagship in Lake Champlain in a blockade against British infiltration south from Canada, according to *The Dictionary of American Naval Fighting Ships*. On September 11, a British brig fired the first salvo, a shot that hit *Saratoga*'s deck, then struck a poultry cage, freeing a gamecock. "The indignant rooster took to his wings and landed in the rigging. Facing the British warships, the cock defiantly called out challenge to battle," the ships dictionary states. Inspired, the American flotilla blasted the British. In the ensuing battle, *Saratoga* suffered losses but eventually captured two ships, forced two others to surrender in the fighting, and made others flee. After the war, *Saratoga* was later sold in New York. Since then, the gamecock has served as a symbol for the series of *Saratoga* ships and is part of the ship's crest.

The third *Saratoga*, a sloop of war, was first commissioned in 1843 and, in her sixty-four-year history, was decommissioned and reactivated a number of times. The ship's first orders took her to the western coast of Africa to protect American citizens and suppress slave trade. For a time, the ship protected freed blacks from America who had settled in a new colony, Liberia. Nearby tribes who had profited by capturing and selling their brethren as slaves were hostile toward the emancipated blacks. In 1845, the *Saratoga* was sent to the Gulf of Mexico to quell tensions brewing between the United States and Mexico over the annexation of Texas. In 1850, the ship sailed to the Far East to protect American interests while a treaty with Japan was drafted and signed. During the Civil War, the ship protected Union shipping trade in the Delaware Bay and was part of a South Atlantic Blockage Squadron off the Carolinas. In her last years, the *Saratoga* served as a training ship for naval apprentices and later as a state marine school.

The fourth ship to carry the name *Saratoga* originally was a cruiser named *New York*. On February 16, 1911, the ship was renamed *Saratoga*. The ship was involved in the Spanish-American War and World War I.

The fifth *Saratoga* was originally laid down as a battle cruiser in 1920, but was ordered converted into an aircraft carrier. It was commissioned by the Navy in 1927. During the years preceding World War II, the ship participated in a number of fleet exercises. Following the Japanese strike on Pearl Harbor on December 7, 1941, *Saratoga* was quickly dispatched to the region. On January 11, 1942, the ship was hit by a Japanese submarine torpedo as it was on its way to rendezvous with the *Enterprise*. Six men were killed and three fire rooms were flooded, but the *Saratoga* reached the Hawaiian island of Oahu under its own power. During World War II operations in the Pacific, the carrier earned seven battle stars, engaged in a number of spectacular strikes, and was struck by enemy fire several times. At the end of the war, *Saratoga* transported 29,204 Navy veterans back from the Pacific — more

The Saratoga *cruises the Mediterranean. (Navy Photo by PH1 Paul D. Goodrich)*

than any other single ship.

After the war, the ship was used in atomic bomb testing at Bikini Atoll. *The Dictionary of American Naval Fighting Ships* offers this description of the demise of the fifth *Saratoga*: "She survived the first blast, an air burst on July 1 [1946] with only minor damage, but was mortally wounded by the second on July 25, an underwater blast which was detonated under a landing craft 500 yards from the carrier. Salvage efforts were prevented by radioactivity, and seven and one-half hours after the blast, with her funnel collapsed across her deck, *Saratoga* slipped beneath the surface of the lagoon."

After the war, as the Navy embarked on a massive aircraft carrier construction program, the second of the *Forrestal*-class ships would bear the name *Saratoga*. With the sixth *Saratoga* taken out of commission August 20, 1994, admirers of the legacy hope one day a new ship will carry on the tradition inspired by a victorious group of early Americans during the Revolution to secure the United States. ▪

The illuminated "60" on the ship's island during Operation Desert Storm. (Navy Photo by PH2 Bruce Davis)

Invincible Fighting Cock

A fighting gamecock is perched atop the crest of the *Saratoga*, ready to attack, beak open wide in defiance. *Invictus Gallus Gladiator*, Invincible Fighting Cock. The gamecock has served as a mascot for Navy ships named *Saratoga* since September 11, 1814, when the second ship named *Saratoga* served as the flagship in a blockade against the British on Lake Champlain. A gamecock, knocked free of its cage by a British cannon shot that struck the *Saratoga*'s deck, stood in the rigging and cawed pugnaciously at the British. Inspired, the crew of the *Saratoga* went on to lead the Americans to victory.

The bird served as a symbol of strength and pride for *Saratoga* crews. In fact, at different times, gamecocks have been housed on board as live mascots. It's not difficult to imagine, however, that the live poultry also was a source of sailor mischief.

In 1956, the CVA-60's first year, a Rhode Island Red fighting rooster was donated to the ship. When the ship made a port visit in Haiti, a chief petty officer managed to enter the bird in a local cockfight. As word of the cockfight grew, sailors packed a Haitian arena to root for their mascot in the duel with the Haitian rooster. American greenbacks and Haitian gourdes stacked up as the betting proceeded. The ship's well-groomed and healthy Rhode Island Red immediately tore into a ragged Haitian bird the instant the two were set in the ring. The Haitian trainer grabbed his wounded bird and held it for a few seconds and put it back in the ring. This time, *Saratoga*'s rooster was scratched and bloodied. The *Saratoga* chief pulled the bird and found that the opposition had put sharp spurs on the legs of the Haitian cock.

All hell broke loose. Haitians and sailors grabbed for the money. Fists flew and shouting erupted. Soon the Haitian police entered carrying swords. The *Saratoga* sailors managed to escape the mayhem. Needless to say, the chief had to answer for taking the bird off the ship and entering it in the fight.

Before President Eisenhower's visit to the ship the next year, mischievous sailors doused a mascot bird with green paint. It quickly fell ill and had to have its feathers plucked to save its life. Later, the chattering

(Official U.S. Navy Photo)

bird annoyed some other sailors who retaliated by tossing it, cage and all, overboard. In an attempt to get the cage-tossing culprit to fess up, ship captain R. D. Moore called the sailors to muster on the flight deck and required them to stand at attention in the hot Caribbean sun for hours. No one came forward. When the ship returned to May-port, the story of the green rooster spread and inspired a singer at a local bar frequented by *Saratoga* sailors to write a song about the misadventure.

Ship mascots were purportedly heaved overboard more than once in the history of the ship. It was finally determined that it was not a good idea to keep a live bird aboard. ◾

On the deck during Operation Desert Shield. (Navy Photo by CWO2 Ed Bailey)

The USS Saratoga *(CV-3) in San Francisco Bay, California. (Official U.S. Navy Photograph)*

The USS *Saratoga* Association

Six years after the USS *Saratoga* (CV-3) was sunk in an atomic bomb test, Bob Portwig, the original wardroom steward of the World War II aircraft carrier, called shipmate Mickey Derach and suggested they put together a reunion for *Saratoga* crew members. Derach agreed to the idea, and they started telephoning other shipmates, among them sailors from the ship's electrical division who had already been meeting for several years. By that fall, 1952, they had assembled a large group, including four admirals and five captains, who met in Long Beach, California, for a social gathering. Forty-three years later, sailors from *Saratoga* (CV-3) continue to meet on an annual basis at different sites around the country to renew friendships and maintain the memory of their illustrious ship. "I've been on thirty-two ships, and *Saratoga* [CV-3] has always been my favorite," said P. R. "Tony" Tonelli, who has served diligently as secretary and treasurer of the USS *Saratoga* Association for thirty-two years.

The association welcomed their brethren from the sixth *Saratoga* (CV-60), and now about a quarter of the association's 2,600 members hail from the supercarrier.

Artifacts from both ships are on display in spaces below the hangar deck on the carrier USS *Yorktown*, the centerpiece of Patriots Point Naval and Maritime Museum in Charleston, South Carolina. Photographs, news clips, flags flown in World War II battles, a model of CV-3, and a uniform from Admiral William Hasley, Jr., commanding officer of CV-3 from July 1935 to June 1937, are exhibited. If the USS *Saratoga* Museum Foundation in Jacksonville is successful in mooring the *Saratoga* (CV-60) as a maritime museum in the city, the memorabilia on board the *Yorktown* will be moved to the ship in Florida.

Harvey Hirsch, Jr., a CV-60 shipmate from the late 1950s, heads up the contingent of shipmates active in the association. The fellowship in the association is incredible, he says. "We were out there and shared the risks as well as the joys," Hirsch said. "It doesn't matter what the ranks of the other men were. If an admiral comes in who served on the ship, he's still a shipmate. Year and rank does not come into play."

For years to come, the association will continue to proudly perpetuate the memory of both aircraft carriers named *Saratoga*. ◼

(Official U.S. Navy Photo)

The USS *Saratoga's* Next Life

Following her commissioning and early sea trials in 1956, the *Saratoga* steamed south from the New York Naval Shipyards at Brooklyn to a newly revived ship basin along the Atlantic Ocean at Mayport, Florida. For the next thirty-eight years, the *Saratoga* called Mayport and its Jacksonville community home. Thousands of sailors brought their families to the community to live while they served on the mighty aircraft carrier. In a ritual repeated over and over, wives and children and other local residents gathered at dockside to wave good-bye when the ship pulled out to sea, then returned months later to greet sailors anxious to be back home. The *Saratoga* became an integral part of the Jacksonville community, a symbol of the strong Navy presence in the economic and daily life of the area. Even non-Navy residents of the region closely followed the ship's activities, whether it served in conflicts or merely sailed the world to show its flag. When the *Saratoga* was involved in victories or tragedies, prominent newspaper headlines and television coverage reflected the community's interest.

The *Saratoga* is the only Navy aircraft carrier to date which remained in the same home port throughout its career. As the ship's operations were coming to a close during the summer of 1994, it was clear the Jacksonville community was not ready to let go. By the ship's decommissioning on August 20, an orchestrated effort to retain the retired aircraft carrier on loan from the Navy was moving full steam ahead. The USS *Saratoga* Museum Foundation, Inc., was created to lead the effort to moor the ship in Jacksonville as a maritime museum, rather than let the ship be hauled to Philadelphia for storage and eventual scrapping.

"The *Saratoga* is as much a part of Jacksonville as anything that is here," said Charlie Sawyer, co-chairman of the museum effort. "It is a magnificent opportunity to have a museum, a memorial, and a tourist destination."

The plan requires hefty funding to convince the Navy that the ship can adequately be set up as a museum. The group faces a formidable goal: raising $5.1 million in start-up money.

Aircraft handlers wait to move a Fighter Squadron 74 (VF-74) F-14A Tomcat. (Navy Photo by Senior Airman Chris U. Putman)

Just a few days after the *Saratoga* returned from its final deployment at the end of June, the Jacksonville City Council voted unanimously to underwrite up to $4.5 million in loans for the project — a safety net in case the foundation funding runs short. A consortium of banks agreed to provide loans if enough money wasn't raised from the community for the initial phases. The group determined to save the *Saratoga* is also exploring the issuing of industrial revenue bonds to pay for the conversion of the ship into a museum. The group is convinced it will be able to operate in the black. What borrowing may be necessary, the group says, will be short-term funding to keep the project moving. The museum foundation has been aggressive in recruiting individuals and companies to participate.

Museum proponents believe thousands of tourists will detour off Interstate 95 on their way into and out of Florida to walk across the more than four-acre flight deck, tour ship spaces, and learn about naval aviation through aircraft on board.

If the museum effort is successful, Jacksonville would join several other U.S. cities with retired Navy vessels on display. In fact, a former *Saratoga* commanding officer, James H. Flatley, III, a retired rear admiral, heads the Patriots Point Naval and Maritime Museum in Charleston, S.C. The WWII-era carrier *Yorktown* is the centerpiece of the complex, which includes the submarine *Clamagore* and the destroyer *Laffey*. The group that runs the USS *Lexington* carrier museum in Corpus Christi, Texas, has been advising the Jacksonville group.

Proponents of the museum effort are optimistic that the Secretary of the U.S. Navy will grant conditional approval of the *Saratoga* museum around December 1, 1994. The group hopes to begin constructing a pier and moorings for the *Saratoga* on the south bank of the St. Johns River in downtown Jacksonville at the beginning of 1995. ∎

The Commanding Officers

Captain Robert J. Stroh
April 14, 1956 — December 1, 1956

Captain R. B. Moore
December 1, 1956 — December 17, 1957

Captain Alfred R. Matter
December 17, 1957 — October 16, 1958

Captain John H. Hyland
October 16, 1958 — November 9, 1959

Captain Allen F. Fleming
November 9, 1959 — November 9, 1960

Captain Roger W. Mehle
November 9, 1960 — November 3, 1961

Captain Valdemar G. Lambert
November 3, 1961 — November 3, 1962

Captain Frederick T. Moore
November 3, 1962 — September 28, 1963

Captain John E. Lacouture
September 28, 1963 — October 2, 1964

Captain Jack M. James
October 2, 1964 — September 2, 1965

Captain Harold F. Lang
September 2, 1965 — October 7, 1966

Captain Joseph M. Tulley
October 7, 1966 — September 7, 1967

Captain John H. Dick
September 7, 1967 — April 4, 1969

Captain Warren H. O'Neil
April 4, 1969 — August 8, 1970

Captain Dewitt L. Freeman
August 8, 1970 — August 7, 1971

Captain James R. Sanderson
August 7, 1971 — February 16, 1973

Captain Louis C. Page
February 16, 1973 — September 12, 1974

Captain Robert F. Dunn
September 12, 1974 — September 11, 1976

(Navy Photo by PH1 P. D. Goodrich)

Captain Charles B. Hunter
September 11, 1976 — February 4, 1978

Captain David E. Frost
August 7, 1986 — March 5, 1988

Captain Edward H. Martin
February 4, 1978 — July 14, 1979

Captain James T. Matheny
March 5, 1988 — April 26, 1990

Captain James H. Flatley, III
July 14, 1979 — October 1, 1981

Captain Joseph S. Mobley
April 26, 1990 — April 18, 1991

Captain Leonard G. Perry
October 1, 1981 — November 11, 1983

Captain James M. Drager
April 18, 1991 — December 9, 1992

Captain John K. Ready
November 11, 1983 — March 26, 1985

Captain Donald A. Weiss
December 9, 1992 — February 20, 1994

Captain Jerry L. Unruh
March 26, 1985 — August 7, 1986

Captain William H. Kennedy
February 20, 1994 — August 20, 1994

Awards and Medals

In her thirty-eight years at sea, the USS *Saratoga* (CV-60) was an influential part of many conflicts around the world and often operated under threatening conditions. The ship and her crew received numerous medals and awards during operations in Vietnam, the Persian Gulf War, the Middle East, and Europe. The *Saratoga* was recognized for its efficiency and readiness to serve when called upon, and was honored for its twenty-two cruises to the Mediterranean Sea.

Navy Unit Commendation
(Two awards) 10–11 October 1985 and 23–29 March 1986

Meritorious Unit Commendation
(Three awards) 17 September – 8 October 1970; 18 May 1972 – 8 January 1973; and 1 October 1979 – 15 November 1980

Battle Efficiency Award
1 January – 31 December 1986

Navy Expeditionary Medal
(Two awards) 7 July – 19 August 1961 and 20 January – 29 March 1986

National Defense Service Medal
(Two awards) May 1972 – January 1973 and January – March 1991

Armed Forces Expeditionary Medal
(Four awards) 17-25 July 1958; 29 July – 11 August 1958; 19 August – 7 September 1958; and 3–20 December 1962.

Vietnam Service Medal
(Ten awards) 6–7 May 1972; 17 May – 22 June 1972; 30 June – 16 July 1972; 27 July – 23 August 1972; 2 September – 19 September 1972; 29 September – 21 October 1972; 25–26 October 1972; 3–8 November 1972; 18 December 1972 – 8 January 1973; and 13–19 January 1973.

Southwest Asia Campaign Medal
(Three awards) 22 August – 21 September 1990; 23 October – 9 December 1990; and 6 January – 11 March 1991.

Sea Service Deployment Ribbon
(Twenty–two forward deployments)

Republic of Vietnam Campaign Medal
May 1972 – January 1973

Saudi Arabia's Kuwait Liberation Medal
January – March 1991

At the decommissioning ceremony. (Courtesy of Diane Uhley)

The Plank Owners

In Navy tradition, a ship's first crew are called plank owners. This terminology has its roots in the first aircraft carriers, which had wooden flight decks. When the flight deck was ready for replacement, each member of the first crew was given an original plank. While aircraft carriers like the latest *Saratoga* (CV-60) have steel flight decks, the term "plank owner" remains a tradition. The following crew was the first to take the *Saratoga* to sea:

COMMANDING OFFICER
Captain Robert J. Stroh

EXECUTIVE OFFICER
Commander James W. McCrocklin

EXECUTIVE STAFF OFFICERS:
Ens. E. A. Brooks, Legal Officer; Ens. L. D. Bryant, Public Information Officer; Cdr. J. J. Burns, Catholic Chaplain; CHSHIPCLK R. J. Hayward, Ship Secretary; CHSHIPCLK H. L. Hoagland, Personnel Officer; Cdr. James McCrocklin; Ens. W. J. Nelson, Assistant Legal Officer; Lt.j.g. R. R. Norris, E. & T. Officer; Lt. D. L. Stephenson, Administrative Assistant; Cdr. W. L. Wolf, Protestant Chaplain.

EXECUTIVE STAFF:
TD2 Anderson, PN3 Anderson, YN2 Anderson, SN Baker, LI3 Bean, YN3 Boich, PN3 Brown, LI3 Burzycki, PN3 Campbell, PH3 Canfield, SN Capone, SN Cole, LI1 Conners, SN Curtis, PN3 Denny, YN2 Dignam, SN Dubail, SA Dunn, PN3 Ernsberger, YN3 Fontana, LI3 Gentile, SN Gester, YN2 Givens, SN Goforth, SN Goldblatt, JO1 Graddick, AN Hansen, SN Hayes, AN Henry, SN Hodgins, YN2 Holton, PN1 Jackson, AA Kales, SN

Kite, TD3 Kotowski, PN3 Krumm, PNC Larson, SN Lent, SN Lewis, SN Luttinen, LI3 Mahoney, SN Majors, LI3 Miller, SN Myers, YN2 Rebar, PN3 Reedy, SA Robbins, FN Russell, SN Sandy, YN3 Seifert, SA Smith, SN Snead, SN Springborn, SN Sullivan, SA Swoboda, SA Tarangelo, AN Undaset, YN3 Wapp, PN2 Waters, FN Wright, PN3 Young, PN1 Yumnit.

MASTER-AT-ARMS FORCE:
BT1 Acton, BM1 Brown, 1C2 Calbi, DC2 Cardwell, EN3 Denmeade, PR1 Fenstermacker, BT2 Formanski, RD3 Jordan, ET3 Just, EM2 Kemp, AO1 Langnau, BM2 Madsen, BM2 Nolan, BMC Ostwalt, AB1 Starrick.

AIR DEPARTMENT

Commander Harry B. Gibbs, Air Officer.

V-1 DIVISION:
Operational control of the flight deck.
Lt. Cdr. Carnahan, CHAVOPTECH Eggeling,
ABC Fisher.

AB3 Adam, AN Amidei, AN Anderson, AB2 Baker, AN Ball, AN Bedinghaus, AN Bergeron, AN Bevins, AN

Boyd, AB3 Brady, AB3 Brown, AB3 Brown, AN Burns, AN Burrow, AB3 Butler, AN Callahan, AN Carter, AA Chase, AB3 Cobb, AA Coleman, AN Collins, AA Columbia, AB3 Conrad, AN Crabb, AN Crabtree, AB2 Crane, AN Degrote, AN Dezulovich, AN Dickerson, AN Dodero, AB3 Downes, AN Dunham, AN Fair, AA Froesel, AB3 Fuller, AN Garner, AB1 Gilbert, AN Gray, AN Harris, AN Haut, AA Hayes, AA Henthron, AN Hicks, AN Hooper, AN Houston, AN Howington, AN Ingraham, AN Iszler, AB3 Johnson, AN Kelly, AB1 Kindley, AN Kordick, AN Kotcher, AB1 Lain, AA Lowe, AN Lukasik, AN Markowitz, AB3 Marquardt, AN Maskel, AB3 Melanson, AB3 Metzger, AN Miller, AN Miller, AN Morad, AB2 Mullins, AN Murphy, AN Nordstrom, AN Olson, AN Overton, AN Pachell, AN Pearson, AB3 Pennamen, AN Plishka, AN Powell, AM3 Puglisi, AN Reineking, AA Roach, AN Roe, AN Scalora, AB1 Scheuer, AN Schommer, AN Schwartz, AB2 Scott, AN Sherfield, AA Shoopman, AN Skinner, AA Smith, AN Smith, AN Smith, AN Spruce, AB2 Stephens, AA Suggs, AN Svendsen, AN Thackery, AB3 Thomas, AN Thomas, AN Thompson, AN Vickers, AN Vuljak, AN Waisanen, AA Waldron, AN Waldvogel, AB2 Wells, AN Wheeler, AN White, AB2 Williams, AN Woodall, AN Workman, AA Wright, AB3 Wright, AB1 Wright, AN Zahakos.

V2 DIVISION:
Responsible for the catapult and arresting gear equipment.

Lt. Cdr. Dulhagen, Lt. Douthett, Lt. Everling, Ens. Zack, ABC Hamersley, ABC Kedrowski, ABC Rivers.

AN Allen, AA Araibian, AN Arbogast, AB3 Arnold, AN Ballard, AA Barbour, AB2 Barchis, AB2 Bardar, AN Beers, AN Benson, AB1 Berry, AB3 Beverly, AN Bolt, AN Bolton, AN Boone, AB3 Bruner, AB1 Burke, AB1 Burns, AB1 Burr, AB1 Cernautan, AN Christopher, AN Clapp, AA Collins, AA Davis, AN DeAngelis, AN Degnan, AA Deziel, AN Dickens, AB3 Dietz, AB2 Doughty, AN Duncan, AN Elliot, AN Farmer, AN Fedyk, AN Feil, AA Finney, AA Fortney, AB3 French, AN Gauger, AB3 Gear, AN Glor, AB3 Gore, AB3 Grace, AB2 Graehling, AN Hansen, AN Harmon, AB3 Harper, AN Hemrick, AA Heuer, AB3 Hilton, AB2 Janik, AA Keating, AN Kline, AN Leonard, AA Lloyd, AN Mabry, AB2 Malinosky, AN Mastromoro, AB1 McLemore, AN McCloskey, AN McComber, AE3 McCraney, AN Moran,

AN Morrill, AN Morris, AN Moynihan, AB3 Mueller, AB2 Mortimer, AB3 Navone, AB3 Pancolli, AB1 Parson, AB2 Paul, AB3 Pearsall, AN Phipps, AB3 Pierce, AB2 Prater, AB1 Presnell, AB2 Randolph, AB2 Repaci, AK3 Robbins, AB3 AB3 Roberts, AB1 Rossignal, AN Rousseau, AE3 Rowles, AB1 Russ, AA Smith, AA Tackett, AB3 Turkett, AB3 Turner, AN Turner, AN Vaughan, AN Vogt, AB2 Weddle, AB1 Welford, AN Wetherell, AA Wilson, AB3 Wisniewski, AN Wolffs, AA Woods, AN Woodworth, AN Wyrick, AA Yates, AB3 Zapp.

V-3 DIVISION:
Hangar deck crew that sent the aircraft up to the flight deck for launch.

Lt. Ulm, ABC Geisendaffer.

AA Adams, AB3 Allen, AN Amberg, AB2 Bakker, AN Bird, AN Bosio, AN Burkeen, AN Burkes, AN Carter, AN Conrad, AA Covington, AN Craig, AB1 Daniels, AN Devine, AN Difrancesco, AB3 Doyle, AN Eubanks, AN Giles, AN Golka, AN Gothay, AN Green, AN Gusewelie, AN Hammes, AA Hoffman, AA Hunt, AA Jenkins, AA Johnson, AN Johnson, AN Kearney, AN Kennedy, AN Kyzer, AN Langford, AB3 Langston, AN Lilly, AN Marchland, AN Matthews, AB3 McGinley, AN McKnight, AN Morris, AN Multinax, AB3 Nash, AN Parks, AN Patton, AA Ratulowski, AN Robinson, AN Santos, AN Schaab, AA Schuzer, AN Smoak, AB3 Sweeney, AB2 Tabb, AN Thiel, AN Trambalski, AN Vallesio, AA Weldon, AA White, AN Willingham, AN Wolf, AN Wolff, AN Zachary.

V-4 DIVISION:
Fueled the aircraft and handled aviation fuel fires.

CHAVMAINTECH Judash, ABC Dunlap, ABC Gillespie.

AN Adams, AN Baird, AB3 Baker, AN Beck, AB1 Blessing, AN Bollenberg, AN Brown, AN Browning, AB1 Burkam, AN Canfield, AN Carter, AN China, AN Conners, AB3 Coughlin, AN Couture, AN Crawford, AN Cummings, AN Davis, AB3 Decker, AN Dellaquila, AN Del Castillo, AN Diebold, AA Dinieri, AN Engel, AN Ezell, AN Finch, AB1 Glidewell, AN Guilliams, AN Hageage, SN Halvorson, AN Hand, AN Harris, AB3 Healea, AN Hodge, AN Houchens, AN Hosey, AN Hurley, AN Iddings, AN Jesky, AN Laveque, AN Love, AN Lusk, AN Madonna, AN Mandyck, AN Martin, AN

Martin, AN McCormick, AN McKinney, AN McIntire, AN Meadows, AN Meads, AB3 Miedema, AN Monette, AN Montgomery, AN Moody, AN Morneau, AN Mummert, AB3 Nipper, AN Noegel, AB3 Norian, AB2 O'Brien, AN Papa, AN Patterson, AN Peterson, AN Powell, AN Ragland, AA Riley, AN Rosenthal, AB3 Rubin, AN Schaffner, AN Scott, AN Selario, AN Sifers, AB3 Smith, AN Stephanski, AA Steward, AN Swoboda, AB2 Taylor, AN Vannata, AN Vecchio, AN Westover, AB1 Wetzel, AN Wycich.

V-5 DIVISION:
Responsible for the function of aircraft weapons.

Lt. Cdr. Frodahl, CHAVORDTECH Elliot, GFC Butcher, GFC Furgueron, AOC Rolan.

GF3 Alvino, AO2 Andrelchik, AN Barr, MN3 Beacham, GF3 Boniella, AO2 Bryant, AO3 Campbell, AO1 Carter, AO2 Chanda, AN Coggins, AO3 Daigrepont, AN Dancy, AO3 Daniels, AA Davenport, AO3 Davis, AN Dilley, AN Dorf, AN Ehrhart, AO2 Elliot, AN Ellis, MN3 Erwin, AO2 Fay, AO1 Fuoco, AO3 Gaynor, AO1 Gladieux, AO2 Goodin, AO1Graceffa, AO2 Hinkle, AA Hubbard, AN Hudson, MN1 Hunt, AO2 Johnson, AO1 Kells, AO3 Kirby, AO2 Kolcow, AO2 Kramer, AN Leahy, AQ1 Lee, AA Leshovisek, AO1 Lucas, AN MacDougall, AO2 Martin, AA McCain, AA McCormick, AO3 McDonald, AO3 McGuire, AO3 McKnight, AA McMullen, AO3 Meek, AO3 Montoto, AN Ortolano, AO3 Pack, AO2 Park, AN Parker, GFAN Parsons, AN Patterson, AN Pearman, AN Petendree, AN Proellochs, AO2 Radcliffe, AO3 Ramsay, AN Rhodes, GF3 Schrock, AO3 Searle, AO2 Shelton, AA Simpson, AN Smith, AN Steele, AA Stover, AO2 Thomann, AO1 Waldron, AN Watters, AO2 White, AO1 Williams, AO3 Zydiak.

V-6 DIVISION:
Repaired the aircraft.

Lt. Cdr. Swint, AVELCTECH Roche, ATC Fleming, AMC Madden, ADC Murray, AEC Richards, ADC Rowe, ADC Welch.

AT3 Amarosa, AN Arledge, AD2 Ashforth, AD2 Bartnik, AT1 Beaver, AD1 Bishop, AN Blomgren, AN Bowen, AA Briner, AN Cariel, AN Carraher, AM3 Clevenger, YN3 Clifford, AD3 Coffey, AN Cohen, PR1 Crothers, AM3 Crain, AM1 Crane, AN Daly, AD2 Davis, AD3 Deal,

AM3 Douglas, AN Drummond, AE2 Duncan, AD3 Feurstein, YN3 Florence, AM1 Gore, AD3 Gottlieb, AD3 Hallmark, AM3 Head, AN Hekman, AD2 Helt, AN Hensley, AN Huffines, AE3 Hummel, AM3 Joy, AN Keane, AT3 Kennedy, AN Krimsky, AN Lambert, AM3 Leady, AM1 Lopes, AD3 Macer, AD1 Marken, AN Maulden, AT3 McMahon, AA Meads, AM2 Milhorn, AN Mitchell, AD1 Player, AA Price, AE1 Pooler, YN2 Riedel, AN Scheadler, AE3 Smith, AM2 Stahl, AN Steward, AA Taylor, AN Thornsby, SN Toman, AN Walker, AM3 Whitaker, AN Williams, AM3 Yannarella.

ENGINEERING DEPARTMENT

The largest department kept the ship operating smoothly.
Commander James D. Small

ENGINEERING OFFICERS:
Lt. j.g. Suriano, Lt. j.g. Kidd, Lt. Rockwell, Lt. Mathis, Lt. Cdr. Cash, Lt. Smith, Lt. Mosley, Ens. Knust, Lt. j.g. McGough, Ens. Allemang, Ens. Lipset, CHSHIPREPTECH Smith, SHIPREPTECH Frazee, Ens. Zerbel, Ens. Catoe, CHMACH Crapps, CHMACH Worley, CHELEC Burns, CHMACH Arnesen.

A DIVISION:
Operated and maintained auxiliary equipment throughout the ship.

Lt. Mosley, Ens. Lipset, CHMACH Arnesen, MMC Blaisure, MMC Hatton, MMC Mathes BTC Wolfe, YNC Gangl.

MM1 Abrams, MR2 Aiken, MM2 Bailey, FN Bartlett, FN Bickel, EN3 Bishop, MMC Blaisure, FN Boburka, MM3 Boepple, YN3 Bohman, FN Boucher, MM3 Breen, MM3 Buboltz, MR2 Bulger, MM3 Burczyk, MR1 Burnett, SN Cannan, MM1 Carmichael, MM2 Cillo, EN3 Coble, MM3 Craven, FA Croft, MM1 Davis, YN2 Dignam, FN Dickman, FN Dupont, FN Elliot, FN Felicia, FA Flagg, MM2 Ford, EN3 Fosmire, MM1 Fox, EN2 Garrett, FA Goedtel, FN Gogolin, FA Gothard, FN Green, MM1 Guillot, FA Hart, MMC Hatton, EN3 Haythe, MR2 Holmes, EN3 Howard, FA Hussing, SN Jaberg, FA Jones, FN Kelley, FA Kersey, FN King, FA Kirkover, FN Knight, MM1 Koenig, FN Komor, MM3 Kotansky, FN Kurcin, FN Lambert, EN2 Laroche, EN3 Lavoie, FN Lee, FA Leonard, FA Lewis, FN Lichtle, FN Lollock, FN Maddux, MMC Masud, MMC Mathes, FN McAleese, MM3 McCabe, MR2 McClure, EN3 McGuire, MR3

Melvan, EN2 Minton, FN Mondaro, FA Monroe, FN Moody, FN Moore, FN Morgan, MM3 Moss, MM1 Mullins, FN Nowell, FN Nunes, MM1 Olson, EN3 O'Reilly, MM3 Ortquist, MM1 Ortlip, EN2 Palmer, MM1 Parfitt, EN3 Pearson, FN Pierce, FN Pitts, MM3 Podwinski, MR2 Polancich, MM2 Raines, FN Reedy, FN Reimann, FN Reis, MM3 Reppond, EN2 Rich, FA Rich, MM3 Riche, MM3 Robbins, FN Robertson, EN2 Rosser, MR2 Rounds, MM2 Rudl, FN Sandlin, MR2 Schmitt, FN Schoener, MM3 Sedlak, FA Seifert, MM3 Sepersky, FN Shively, MM3 Siracusa, FN Sivick, EN3 Skol, MM3 Smallman, MM3 Smith, MM3 Smith, EN2 Still, FN Stimmel, FN Theriault, FN Todd, FN Tuhn, FN Ward, MM2 Webb, EN3 Wheeler, MM2 Williams, FN Winegard, FA Wynne, FN Yeargin, FN Zito.

B Division:
Operated the high-pressure steam
equipment and supplied the high-pressure steam for
the propulsion turbines.
They also distilled the water and stored
and distributed the ship's fuel oil.
Lt. j.g. Suriano, Ens. Allemang, CHMACH S. Worley, BTC Black, BTC Brinkley, BT3 Depoy, BTC Diario, BTC Flanagan, BTC Harned, BTC Maiuro.

BTFN Anders, FA Andrews, BT3 Ashley, BT2 Bailey, FN Baldwin, BTFN Bassett, FN Bateman, FA Boulet, BT2 Bell, BT1 Brown, BT3 Brownie, FA Bruhnke, FA Buechler, BT3 Byrd, BT3 Camden, BT3 Carr, BT3 Carroll, BT3 Cienava, BT3 Colepaugh, BT1 Crabtree, FA Crawford, FN Davis, BTFN Deo, BT1 Dembin, FN Douglas, BT2 Dunn, BT1 Dye, BT2 Elvin, BT3 Errico, FN Exford, BT3 Fidler, FN Fokkens, BT3 Goldstein, FN Gordon, BT3 Grimes, FA Grooms, FA Guldenstein, FN Guthridge, FA Hall, FA Hamm, BTFN Hammonds, FA Harrington, FN Heskett, FN Hetrick, BTFN Hewett, BT2 Hickman, FA Hirsch, BT2 Hocking, FA Hoke, BTFA Jackson, FN Jackson, BT3 Jacobs, BT3 Johnson, BT1 Johnson, BT3 Keenan, BT3 Kirst, BT3 Kleiner, FN Kock, FA Krokus, BTFN Labiento, FN Lange, FA Lashway, BTFN Leitner, FA Lewis, BTFN Lindsey, FA Lineberry, BT3 Lyke, BT2 MacDougall, FA Maillet, BTC Maiuro, BTFN Mangels, BTFN McCaffery, BT2 McGuire, FN McKeown, BT3 Mellor, BT2 Mestas, BT2 Milachek, BT3 Moser, BT1 Murphy, BT3 Nemath, BT3 Nickerson, BT3 Oakes, BT3 Oberst, BT2 O'Brien, FA O'Connor, FN Owen, BTFN Paden, FA Palmer, FN Rich, FN Richards, BT3 Sarafin, BTFN Scarafiotta, FA Shorey, FN Sisko, SN Sollner, BTFN Speidel, BT3

Sprossel, BT2 Staffin, FN Steers, BT3 Stevens, FN Steward, FN Steward, BTFN Stewart, BT3 Taipp, BT3 Tomlinson, FA Toth, FN Tritt, BT3 Troyan, BTFN Vendetta, FN Vitale, BTFN West, BT1 Whipple, BT1 Whitaker, BT3 White, BT3 Wiltshire, BTFN Windham, BT3 Winslow, BTFN Wolf, BT3 Young, FN Youngblood, FN Zuidoma.

E Division:
Supplied the electrical power and main generators
and electric plant.

Ens. Zerbel, Lt. Smith, CHELEC Burns, EMC Miller, ICC Kingsbury, EMC Cabaday, EMC Dobbins.

IC2 Abele, EMFN Albert, FN Cecchini, EM3 Bailey, IC1 Baird, EMFN Beatty, EM2 Beljanski, EM2 Bernd, IC3 Berry, IC2 Black, EM1 Bogen, EM1 Branson, EMFN Bridgeman, EM3 Brown, FN Buell, FN Burkinshaw, EM2 Butcher, IC3 Campbell, EM1 Carr, IC3 Cavanaugh, FN Cecchini, FN Chapasko, EM3 Chapman, EM2 Collins, FN Conklin, EM1 Cooper, EM1 Cornelius, FN Costello, EM3 Cottier, IC3 Davis, Dean, EM2, IC3 Decoursey, FN Decueninck, EM3 Dorrer, EMFN Duke, EM3 Edwards, EM3 Ferrara, EM3 Fietkiewicz, IC3 Filippelli, EM3 Finrock, EM1 Forrester, EM2 Freeman, EM2 Frey, EM2 Froutz, EM1 Fuller, IC3 Gardner, ICFN Gentry, IC3 Gildard, EM1 Gillece, FA Gorman, EM1 Gower, EM3 Hagen, EM3 Hammack, EM2 Hare, IC2 Harper, IC2 Harrington, EM2 Harris, EM3 Hartung, IC3 Hernandez, FN Herring, FN Hinson, FN Hoebee, FA Hurley, EMFN Iffland, EM2 James, EM3 Jelinek, EM3 Johnson, IC1 Kelley, EM2 Kosik, EM3 LaBranche, FN La Marche, EM3 Lanier, IC3 Larson, EM3 Lewis, FA Liberty, FA Lochner, FN Maas, EM1 Machala, IC3 Maidment, FN Manthey, FN Mathieson, EM3 Massey, FN McArdle, EM1 McDaniels, IC2 McIntyre, IC3 McKeon, FA McLaughlin, IC3 McPherson, EMFN Mendonca, IC3 Mickiewicz, EM2 Miller, EM2 Milligan, EM3 Misco, EM3 Morey, EM3 Murphy, FN Neilson, IC3 Neuman, EM2 Novak, IC2 O'Dell, FA O'Hara, EM3 Paul, EM3 Peck, FN Perry, FA Petroski, EM3 Rawlings, EM3 Reed, IC3 Reese, EM2 Reeves, EM1 Regan, EM2 Riess, FN Roberts, EM1 Root, IC2 Schaffer, EMFN Schatzel, EM2 Schneider, FA Schoonover, FN Schwartzlow, EM1 Sekelsky, IC2 Shagogue, FN Shanks, EM3 Sharkey, FA Skelly, EM1 Smith, EM3 Smoot, ICFN Star, EM3 Sumption, EM3 Switzer, EM2 Thomas, EM3 Tuchenhagen, FA Underwood, EMFN Verchereau, EM3 Wall,

FN Walsh, EM3 Warrington, EM2 Weatherford, IC2 Whelan, FA Williams, EM3 Woll, EM2 Yarter.

M DIVISION:
Maintained the main engines, turbines, and electric turbo-generators that kept the ship moving.

Lt. Rockwell, MMC Disotell, MMC Healy, Ens. Catoe.

FN Adkins, FA Alexander, MM3 Anderson, MM2 Ault, MM3 Bauer, MM2 Bazelka, MM3 Beaudoin, MM3 Belcher, FN Bermel, FN Berry, FA Blaisure, FN Brosi, MM3 Burger, FA Burgess, FN Burkey, MM1 Cardinal, FN Carey, MM3 Chireau, FN Clarke, FN Cline, MMFN Cole, FA Cox, MM3 Crews, MM3 Crickmore, FN Crippin, MMFA Cunning, FN Curry, MM3 Day, FN Derrera, FA Devine, FN Dugger, FN Dunn, MM3 Eaves, MML3 Ellis, MM1 Ellisor, MM3 Fager, MMFN Forcier, FN Ford, MM2 Frum, FA Futrell, MM3 Garvin, FN Goudreau, MM1 Grassel, FN Hagan, FN Hanson, MM1 Healey, MMFN Hearth, MM3 Hespe, FA Higginbotham, FA Hockfield, FN Holder, FA Hunter, FA Jackson, FN Johns, FN Johnson, FN Johnson, MM2 Johnston, FA Jones, FA Jones, FN Jones, MM3 Jones, MM3 Kemp, MMFN Lemaire, MM3 Lovett, FA MacDonald, FN Marotto, FN Matthews, FA McGuire, MM3 Moody, FA Munday, FA Osorio, MM3 Picciano, MM3 Polasky, MMFN Pongracz, MM2 Popper, MM1 Price, FA Ragland, FA Rapaport, MM1 Riggs, MM3 Ringer, FA Robel, FA Rosado, FA Rupp, FN Saladino, MR3 Schoenfeld, FN Sciotto, FN Shapiro, FN Singleton, FN Steis, FN Sullivan, MM1 Tate, FA Taylor, FN Theibotot, FN Torgrimson, FN Torres, MM1 Vaughn, FN Wallis, FA Wheeler, MM1 White, MM2 Wilkinson, MM3 Williams, MM3 Wilson, FN Woodlief.

R DIVISION:
Repaired leaks, maintained hatches and doors, and made up the backbone of the fire-fighting force.

Lt. j.g. Kidd, CHSHIPREPTECH Smith, SHIPREPTECH Frazee, DCC Lindsey, MEC Southerland.

FA Absher, ME3 Allrutz, ME3 Anyder, FN Atkins, ME3 Bergeron, FN Blackburn, FN Bodmer, FA Boyd, ME3 Bremm, DC1 Bryant, DC2 Burch, DC2 Cain, FP2 Chicky, ME3 Christian, DC2 Christoffersen, FN Clarkson, FN Crawford, FN Cross, ME3 Davis, DC1 Denny, FP2 DeYoung, DC2 Duckworth, FP3 Dunston,

FP3 Emmi, DC1 English, ME1 Franklin, DC3 Fulk, DC3 Gable, DC2 Gamache, FP3 Glover, FA Goocher, FP3 Greer, FP2 Gregory, ME2 Greim, FN Hafner, FN Haight, FN Hall, DC1 Hall, ME2 Hellams, FP3 Hennessey, FN Holcomb, DC3 Holmes, DC2 Hoyle, FN Hupp, DC2 Ives, FP3 Kelley, DC2 Larsen, DC2 Latimore, ME2 Lilly, FN Linde, FN Lipton, FN Mansfield, ME3 Martin, FN Maske, FN Maxwell, FN Mazzarietto, FA McLain, FN Melton, FN Messman, FN Michalowksi, FN Miller, FN Moore, FN Morell, FN Murphy, FA Myers, ME3 Negrelli, FP1 Northington, FP2 Peelish, FA Peterson, DC1 Petitt, FA Pfarr, DC2 Phillips, DC2 Phillips, DC2 Rawls, FP1 Rhodes, RA Rogers, ME2 Sammons, FN Sandoval, FN Sawyer, ME3 Schaffer, FA Spoonemore, FN Sprinkle, FN Stiernagle, FP2 Stroud, FN Thiac, FP2 Thompson, DC2 Vandal, FP2 Vissering, FA Walker, FA White, ME2 Wilson, FN Woodruff, FA Wright, FN Zeitler.

GUNNERY

Commander George L. Block
Divisions 1 through 4 handled anchors, fueling and replenishing, rigging and gangways, manning boats, operating boat booms, and assisted in mooring.

1ST DIVISION:
Lt. j.g. Signor, Ens. Crossman, CHBOSN Angeroth, BMC O'Donnell.

AM2 Anderson, SN Anderson, SN Arms, SA Arms, SN Barrera, SN Bassler, BM2 Blanchette, SN Blum, SN Booth, SA Bosley, SN Brown, SN Burgess, BM3 Burke, SA Caricato, SA Carson, SA Childers, SN Clum, SA Curtis, SA Davis, SN Delimater, SA Dial, SA Diotte, BM2 Evans, SN Fazio, BM3 Fendley, SA Fraze, SN Fryar, AN Hester, SN Hubener, SN Izzo, SN Johnson, SA Leraan, SN Long, SN Lynch, SN Lynch, SN Martinez, SN McAndrew, BM3 McKenzie, BM2 McMasters, SA McNally, BM3 McSweeney, SA Miklica, SA Moroney, BM3 Page, SA Phillips, SA Poebles, SN Porter, SA Proveaux, SA Rhodes, SA Roman, SN Rosser, FA Rossiter, SN Ruperto, BM1 Saucier, SA Sickles, SA Smith, SN Steadman, BM3 Stevenson, SN Tevault, SA Tillitson, BM3 VanDeren, SN Vogelsang, SN Wagemann, SN Washburn, SN Waters, BM2 Watkins, FA Watkins, SN Wedeles, SN Whitechair, SN Williams, SN Windsor, BM1 Wortham, SN Wright, BM1 Ziegler.

2nd Division:
Lt. Barto, Ens. Pope.

SA Auls, SA Baken, SA Banning, SA Blackley, SA Blake, SA Beard, SA Bentley, SA Brim, SA Brooks, SN Brown, SA Clark, SA Clark, SA Close, BM3 Cooke, BM2 Critzer, SA Crump, BM1 Cusick, SA Dorrell, SA Emberton, SN Emory, SN Evans, SA Feiler, SA Fernandez, BM2 Fisher, SA Frederick, SA Fuller, SN Gambardella, SA Geving, SA Green, SA Hanslin, SA Harper, BM3 Harper, BM1 Heine, SN Humiston, SA Jenkins, SA Jones, SA Jordon, BM2 Kane, BM1 King, SA Kline, SN Lewis, SA Lewis, BM3 Logan, BM2 Luna, SA Lutz, SN Lyons, SN Markiewicz, SA Maurer, SA McCurdy, SA McKinney, BM3 Morgan, SN Odom, SK3 Ozieozic, SN Pugh, SA Quinn, SN Rhodes, SA Riggio, SA Rodriguez, SA Rosenberger, SA Seisputowski, SA Sellito, SA Smith, SN Smith, SA Stegall, SA Stevens, SA Summers, SA Tomai, SN Vermilye, SN Walker, BM3 Wallace, SA Warren, BM2 Weidner, SN Wilkins, SA Willman, SA Woronecki, BM3 Wuertenberg.

3rd Division:
Lt.j.g. McPhail, Ens. Rodgers, BMC Clifton.

YN3 Ambler, SN Cale, SA Crittendon, SN Dieffenback, SA Distrola, SA Donald, SN Duda, SN Eller, SA Few, SN Forney, SN Foster, SA Gibson, SA Goldnick, SN Gomez, SN Gregor, SN Hammond, SA Haney, BM3 Hart, SN Heacox, SN Hendren, SA Hickey, SA Holmes, SA Hudgins, SN Knox, BM3 Kolk, SN Lacy, BM1 Ladd, SN Lee, SN Leffew, SN Levin, SA Lyons, SN Mallett, SA Martinez, SN McCaskill, SA Merritt, SN Mooney, BM3 Montgomery, BM3 Morris, SA Oddo, SA Palozola, SA Pantone, BM3 Rafferty, SN Rebman, SA Scarberry, SA Scheingold, SN Shearer, SA Sifford, BM1 Sites, SA Soliday, SA Spencer, BM1 Spurrell, SN Stegall, SN Strack, SN Sullivan, SA Valentine, SN Vince, SN Webb, SA Webster, SA White, SN Wiekman, SN Wiggins, SN Winchell, SN Wolfe, SA Woodward, BM3 Wytcherley, SN Yearly, SA Yost.

4th Division:
Lt. Gorman, Ens. Lighton.

BM3 Adams, SA Arcand, SN Albright, SN Barnes, SA Beller, SA Boscarino, SA Botterbusch, BM2 Branton, SA Breauit, SA Brooks, BM3 Canestra, SA Cantrell, SA Chenoweth, SA Collett, BM3 Cook, BM3 Cornell, SN Curroa, SN Davis, SA Diana, BM1 Dixon, SA Eshman,

SN Evers, SA Floyd, SN Geisel, SA Goodrich, BM1 Forrester, BM3 Harding, SN Hayden, SN Heri, SA Isom, SA Jackson, BM3 Jarrett, SN Johnson, BM2 Lemay, SN Leshon, SN Lapointe, SA Lloyd, SA Lowe, SA Madden, SN Martin, SA Matthews, SA Melton, SN Miller, SA Mixon, SA Moore, SA Moses, SN Neff, SA Nieforth, SA Nilsen, SN Norris, SA Osborne, SA Peart, SN Perry, SN Plows, BM3 Pool, SN Prime, SN Rasmussen, BM3 Rimmele, SA Rivord, SA Robertson, BM2 Ross, SN Schroeder, SN Schaffner, BM2 Sharpe, SA Simms, SA Sinks, SA Smith, BM1 Smith, SN Smith, SA Snow, SA Stabinsky, BM3 Telken, BM3 Thomas, SN Vance, SN Vigar, SN Walsh, SA Wilson, SA Workman.

5th Division:
Operated the 5-inch battery operations to keep the ship safe from air attack.

Lt.j.g. Babcock, Ens. Sherk, GMC Cooke, GMC Henry. GM2 Blatnik, GM3 Bradley, GM3 Brandon, GM1 Brown, GM2 Charlton, GM1 Clark,

SN Corvi, SA Daniels, GM3 Demars, SA Derr, GM3 Doerler, SN Eakins, GM3 Epperson, SN Floyd, GM2 Gonzales, SN Habben, GM3 Holland, SA King, SA Kmetz, GM3 Kruse, GM1 Lacey, GM1 Moppin, SA Morgan, SA Morris, GM3 Neal, SN Nickle, SN Johnston, GM3 Parsons, SN Pratt, SN Randall, SA Rohanna, GM3 Rollins, SA Sanford, GM3 Shafer, SN Siess, GM3 Siler, SN Stearns, SA Swarhout, SA Taylor, SA Tumlin, SN Wencl, SN Wellman, SN Wesley, GM1 Willi.

6th Division:
Kept watch over the ship's armories and magazines.

Lt. Carter, Lt.j.g. Granger, CHSUROROTECH Deibner, GMC Cole.

SA Bailey, SN Bissonnette, SN Blasingame, SA Boyd, GM2 Brown, GM2 Bryce, SA Canfield, SN Chandler, SN Choppa, SN Coward, SN Dean, YN2 Digilio, SA Edwards, SA Evans, YN1 Flora, SN Fargraf, GM3 Gibson, SN Gould, SA Gue, SN House, SN Hunt, GM3 Huss, SN Kacprazak, GM1 Kavanagh, GM3 Koller, SA Kruger, SN Lanieri, SN Laytart, SN Lohrenz, SN Marsyada, SA McCloud, SN Miller, SA Mullens, GM2 Pipa, SN Purnell, CM3 Radtke, SN Sabo, GM1 Schnell, SN Sellers, GM2 Siegerdt, GM3 Stelmack, YN2 Supek, SN Taylor, SA Thomas, SA Terry, SN Tokach, SA Vollmer, SN Webb, SN Weber, SN Whitehead, SN Wyant, SN Zarowsky.

F DIVISION:

Fire controlmen prepared to fire at rapidly moving aircraft. They operated equipment such as range finders, computers, fire control radar, and director switchboards.

Lt. Deacon, Ens. Brandel,
CHORDCONTECH Fields, FTC Cahill, FTC Hornsby,
FTC Maslo.

SN Allen, SN Baird, SN Bedard, FT2 Black, FT3 Blais, FT3 Bonnin, SA Case, SA Cummings, FT3 Danes, SN Erisman, FT3 Fatula, FT2 Force, FT3 Furbish, SN Giemont, SN Godissart, FT2 Gomez, SN Griep, SN Harvey, FT3 Krovisky, SN Leach, SA Longo, FT2 Love, FT3 Mack, SN Martellota, SN Occhipinti, SN Phelps, SN Purdy, FT1 Thomas, FT2 McIntosh, FTSN Reynolds, FT3 Roberts, FT2 Schuler, FT3 Sour, SN Tagge, FT2 Tomko, SA Wiesebann, FT1 Woodall, FT2 Yelavich, FT3 Zellin.

7TH DIVISION:

The Marine Detachment.
Capt. Quinn, 1st. Lt. Fortune, Master Sgt. Johnson,
Staff Sgt. Ferriter, Sgt. Lance,
Sgt. Schaffer.

Pfc. Atkinson, Pfc. Bacon, Pfc. Boos, Pfc. Burk, Pfc. Brinkley, Cpl. Bryant, Cpl. Coon, Pvt. Corvello, Pfc. D'Amato, Pfc. Dickerson, Cpl. Doerr, Pvt. Downing, Pfc. Dube, Elbe, Pfc. Falta, Cpl. Flowers, Pvt. Ferguson, Pvt. Gallien, Pfc. Gambol, Pfc. Gimblet, Pfc. Gross, Pfc. Gypin, Pfc. Halloran, Pfc. Hiller, Pfc. Hunter, Pfc. Jobson, Pfc. Johnson, Pfc. Johnson, Pvt. Jones, Cpl. Kelley, Pfc. Kennedy, Pfc. Lambert, Pfc. MacDonald, Cpl. Mathews, Pfc. McNamara, Pfc. Melanson, Pfc. Metzger, Pfc. Miko, Pfc. Mitchell, Pfc. Moiser, Cpl. Moody, Pfc. Moseman, Pfc. Mutka, Pfc. Nemits, Pfc. Pochron, Pfc. Perkowski, Cpl. Rapoza, Pfc. Saffron, Cpl. Schreiner, Pvt. Segreve, Pfc. Sobrano, Pvt. Soldo, Pfc. Steiner, Pfc. Thowless, Pfc. Tustin, Pfc. Voyer, Pvt. Wade, Cpl. Warner, Pfc. Weissinger, Pfc. Yasvin, Pfc. Zurawski.

W DIVISION:

Assembled special weapons.

Lt. Cdr. Henri, Lt. Cdr. Cupp, Lt.j.g. Alles, Lt.j.g. Schaefer, Lt.j.g. Pixley, Ens. Burkelman, Ens. Glass, Ens. Regan, Ens. Sundius, EMC Cook, AOC Hawkins, AOC Joy, ETC Russell, EMC Scriber, EMC Slobodny. ME2

Bailey, GM2 Battan, ET1 Catron, ET2 Chesney, GM2 Clark, EM1 Darling, EM1 Dutton, AO2 Earp, ET2 Grenon, SN Guenther, GM3 Hambley, AO1 Harrell, MR2 Hoy, GM1 Isaacs, SK1 Johnson, AO1 Kuhns, EM2 Malia, SN Margis, AO2 Medary, ET1 Miller, GM1 Paupore, GM2 Ramsden, AO1 Robbins, ET2 Rothe, EMFN Skipworth, EM2 Vestal, EM1 Warford, ET1 Weber, EM3 Wisniewski, YN1 White, AO1 Wood.

MEDICAL DEPARTMENT

The medical department on the *Saratoga* could handle any illness, including major surgery.

Captain Sidney I. Brody.

H DIVISION:

Lt.j.g. Drake, HMC McNeil, HMC Williams. HM2 Bee, HM2 Bundrant, HM2 Deberry, HM2 Handeland, HM3 Harris, HM3 Harrison, HN Hess, HM1 Holifield, SN Houle, HM2 Kosloski, HN Kuhns, SA Lehman, HM2 Lita, HM1 Lockett, HM1 Madden, HM2 Martin, HM3 Massengill, HM1 McCarter, HM1 Meyer, HN Morello, HM3 Nolte, HM1 Rolf, HM2 Smith, HM2 Szabo, HM2 Tyler, HM3 Ubl, HM3 Vines, SN Winkler, HM3 Yorka, HM2 Zurbrigen.

NAVIGATION

At the helm, they steered the ship to distant ports and plotted the ship's course and position.

Navigation Officer Commander
Chester D. Rogers.

Lt. Crawford, QMC Sawaniewski.

SN Ashmore, SN Boswell, SN Bradford, QM3 Butler, QMSN Carlson, QMSN Cates, SN Cooper, QM2 Daniels, QM2 Fraiser, QM2 Jones, QM2 LaBranche, QMSN Lascelle, QM1 Lewis, QM3 Lockhart, SN Lockwood, QM2 Morris, QM2 Myers, SN Nozzarella, QM1 Porter, QM3 Rees, QM3 Tarsi, YN3 Thompson, YN2 Werner.

OPERATIONS

Commander Raymond E. Moore
OA DIVISION: The weathermen were responsible for forecasts over both sea and land.

Lt. Reider, AGC Boucher.

AG3 Ainslie, AG3 Clegg, AN Deutsch, AG3 Ehrhard, AG3 Ercole, AG2 Folek, AG3 Friel, AG3 Mangan, AG2 Matlack, AG3 Mikulski, AN Moment, AG1 Nemcosky, AN Powers, AG3 White, AGAN Wimmer, AG2 Zahoranacky.

OI Division:
Manned the Combat Information Center and Air Plot, keeping combat and tactical information up to date.
Cdr. Stanley, Lt. Blaschka, Lt. Blizzard, Lt. Miller, Lt. Vollmer, Lt. Warwick, Lt.j.g. Bradbury, Lt.j.g. Brown, Ens. Bryant, Ens. Hayden, RDC Holland, RDC Warlikowski.

SN Adams, SA Allen, SN Asbell, SN Aube, SN Beckwith, SN Belval, SN Branson, RD2 Bremer, RD3 Brickner, SN Buckworth, SN Castner, RD3 Cantelmo, RD3 Cerami, SA Crowder, SA Delk, SN Douglas, RD3 Dragoivts, RD2 Eller, SN Faust, SN Fikes, RD2 Finegan, SN Flory, SA Fryer, RD3 Golder, RD3 Goldman, SN Haber, RD3 Hay, YN3 Hummel, AC2 Johnston, SA Kosbau, RD3 Lafonte, RD2 Langenwalter, AN Lee, SN Leonard, RD3 Long, RD3 Mallory, RDSN Melnick, RDSN Miller, RD3 Milligan, AB3 Minor, SN Moreau, SN Morris, SN Morrow, SN Myers, SN Patrick, SN Perrault, RD3 Petty, SN Phelps, SA Reed, RD3 Reisert, RD3 Ricks, AN Rosemeyer, SN Russo, SN Santora, SN Savas, RD3 Scheller, SA Shaban, SN Slaughter, SN Snively, RD3 Snyder, RD3 Sobek, RD3 Stuart, SN Synczyszyn, AN Taggart, RD3 Tolson, RD1 Torrey, SA Tracy, RD3 Tully, RD3 VanMoppes, SN Wassel, RD1 Williams, SN Willis, RD3 Wood.

OR Division:
Received and transmitted all radio and teletype communications.

Cdr. DeBord, Lt.j.g. Fowkes, Lt.j.g. Mercer, Lt.j.g. Smyth, RMC Brinkley.

RM3 Allen, TESN Arragon, RMSN Baeder, RM2 Baker, TE3 Bunce, RM3 Capadano, TE1 Chierici, RM2 Collins, RM3 Coogle, TE3 Crowley, RM3 Derock, SN Ferguson, TE3 Fritz, TE2 Giroux, RM1 Graham, RMSN Grant, TE3 Jeffers, RM3 Kolodziejczyk, RMSN Kresse, RMSN Lent, RM3 Muccio, RMSN Paulison, TE1 Pringnitz, TE2 Roberts, RM3 Russek, TE3 Santoro, SM1 Scales, TE3 Tetreault, TE1 Tolliver, TESN

Vaughan, RMSN Walsh.

OS Division:
The signalmen handled all forms of visual communications, from flags to semaphore.

Ens. Warren, SMC Raduns.

SM1 Beers, SM3 Bowe, SN Brahe, SA Brown, SA Demattia, SM3 Fairbanks, SM1 Fowler, SN Garber, SM3 Gillis, SN Golock, SA Hall, SN Hodo, SN Poffenberger, SN Reth, SN Sande, SM3 Thompson, SN Turner.

OP Division:
The photographers recorded all official happenings on the ship and handled aerial photography.

PHOT Burton, PHC Robinson.

PH3 Ainslie, AN Ballo, PHAN Bechle, SN Biddle, PH3 Bowen, AN Goodman, SA Gulley, PHAN Higdem, AN Johnston, PH2 Maas, PH1 Marbut, SN Martens, SA Mogil, AN Noble, YNSN Okler, SA Price, PH3 Rau, YN3 Smith, PH3 Stanley, PH3 Stevenson, SN Tanis, YN2 Tardio, AN Tome, SA Wade, SA Williams.

OE Division:
The electronics technicians kept all the ship's electronic gear running.

Lt. McGowan, Ens. Kirby, CHELCTECH Blum, ETC McGuire, ETC Monthie, ETC Thomas.

ET3 Backowski, ET3 Barnes, ET3 Barrigan, ETSN Bates, ET2 Briscoe, ET2 Burlingame, ET3 Caplinger, ET3 Cardinal, ET2 Donbrowski, ET3 Dube, ET3 Durgee, SN Hallman, ET2 Jones, ET2 Jones, SN Kaplan, ET3 Kitchner, SA Kramer, ET2 Licence, ET1 Lowe, SN Luther, SA Michalsky, SN Miller, SA Mills, ET1 Moorcroft, SN Nitzsche, ET3 Rainey, ET3 Russell, SA Seferlis, ET3 Simons, ET2 Strachan, BT3 Vance, ET3 Volland, ET1 Ward, SN Woodberry.

SUPPLY
_____

Commander Lawrence Lovig, Jr.

S-1 Division:
Requisitioned stores and kept the ship supplied with necessities ranging from electrical parts to

official forms for administration.

Lt. Cdr. Yearick, Lt. Caliman, SKC
Henninger, SKC March, SKC Murray.

SN Adkins, SKSN Agard, SA Atherton, SN Bailey, SN
Bergklint, SK3 Byers, SK2 Carroll, SK3 Cormier, SK2
Davenport, SN Dawson, SA Denny, SN Dietrich, SK3
Doerr, SN Eroh, SK3 Fiskum, SK3 Flahiff, SK2 Flores,
SN Fox, SN Gately, SK1 Gilroy, SA Goad, SA Green,
SN Jones, SKSN Letze, SA Linkus, SK3 Loeffler, SK3
Lymburner, SN Maki, SN Mason, SN McCarty, SK3
McGregor, SN McQueen, SN Moosebrugger, AN Murray,
SN Pilkauskas, SK3 Rigoni, SN Ridz, SA Robinson,
SK3 Ross, SN Sabino, SN Saxon, SK1 Simons, SN
Stockhammer, SA Tice, SA Triplett, SA Vettor, SN
Warner, SA Watkins, SA Whipple, SK3 Yarnell.

S-2 DIVISION:
Cooks, bakers, and commissary experts
fed the entire crew.

Cdr. Lovig, CHSUPCLK Vinson, CSC Piver, CSC Reid,
ABC Shaw. SN Archer, N Artis, FA Bastedo, SN
Baylor, SA Beck, BM1 Bergmann, CS2 Bledsoe, SA
Bohn, ME3 Bonenfant, CS3 Boone, SN Borgerhoff, CS2
Braxton, CS3 Bronson, SA Bringsplenty, CS3 Brown,
CS3 Browning, SA Bucshon, SA Caldwell, SN Cauthen,
MML3 Chester, SA Childers, CS2 Cobb, SA Cornelison,
FA Corrao, SA Creighton, CS2 Cross, SN Crudele,
RDSN Cullom, CS3 Davenport, SA Davis, CS2
DeBellevue, CS2 Delaney, SA Diotte, CS2 Doherty, SN
DuBuque, SA Ellison, FA Farrell, CS2 Faust, AA Fawley,
RMSN Fenton, SN Franklin, FA Frederick, FA Gillespie,
BT3 Grant, BT3 Grant, A Green, AN Harper, FA Harrigan,
SN Harrigan, SA Hayes, CS3 Herrera, AA Hines, FA
Hoke, SK3 Houston, FN Howell, SA Hower, CS3
Husk, SA Jaffe, SN Jewell, CS3 Johnson, CS3
Kaczanowski, SN Kent, CS2 Klein, AN Korkes, AA
LaMontagne, AN LaMontagne, FA Liberty, AN
Linebarger, SN Loewenberg, SN Ludwig, FA Lynch,
FN May, CS1 McCrary, SN McKoy, AN McMahdn,
CS2 Mezo, CS3 Miles, SC2 Miller, CS3 Mitchell, SN
Moore, CS2 Morrill, FA Morris, CS3 Nagel, SK1
Navarra, SN Nozzarella, SN O'Hara, SN O'Neill, CS3
Owens, CS3 Payne, SA Peebles, SN Penny, AN Price,
SK2 Prior, CS3 Rankin, AA Ray, SK3 Reardon, AN
Reid, AN Rice, SN Rickert, TE2 Ritenour, FA Rosado,
CS3 Ruby, SA Runions, SA Russell, FA Russell, SN
Salines, FN Scheller, AN Sherman, SN Sherman, CS3

Skyles, SN Smith, SN Smith, SA Smith, SN Snyder,
CS3 Stamos, AN Starner, SN Stockwell, CS3 Storrie,
SA Stubblebine, SA Swift, SN Swift, SN Thompson, SA
Thomsen, MM3 Thomson, CS3 Tofil, FA Trower, BTFA
VanDyke, CS1 Varcardipone, AN Vyuerberg, CS1
Watson, CS3 Watts, CS3 Waznckewitz, CS2 Williams,
MM3 Wirth, CS3 Wisby, CS3 Wright, CS1 Wynn.

S-3 DIVISION:
Operated barber shops, shoe repair, laundry and dry
cleaning, tailor shops, ship stores, and soda fountains.

Lt. Veazey, Lt.j.g. McCahon, SHC Tisdale.

SA Adams, SA Alston, SK1 Ayers, SH3 Balthazor, SK3
Beaver, SK3 Buschon, SH3 Ciriello, SA Costello, SA
Covington, SA Craft, SH3 Crawford, SH2 Davis, SA
Dinkins, SA Enz, SN Etchinson, DCG3 Fallbright, SH3
Fisk, SH3 Foreman, SH2 Fox, SH3 Gill, SN Gonzales,
SK2 Hadley, SH3 Hanawalt, SH3 Healy, SH3 Hill, SA
Hoover, SA Idoni, SN Jackson, SN Jarm, SA Kegley, SN
Lariviere, SH2 Maddox, SK3 McElroy, SA McNeilly, SA
Miller, SN Ramsey, SH1 Renik, SN Rubino, SA Rushing,
SH2 Rutherford, SN Poboy, SH2 Poortvliet, SH3 Scott,
SN Sebastian, SA Sipple, SH1 Stanton, SH1 Turner,
SK3 Thomas, SA Ulrich, SH3 Williams, SA Williams,
SH3 Yarski.

S-4 DIVISION:
Passed out paychecks and greenbacks.

Ens. McClellan, DKC Crowder, DKC Cowdrey.

DK3 Cina, DK1 Giacin, AN Golden, DK3 Jackson,
DK2 Malabanan, SA McCrann, SN Rosenbalm, DK2
Smith, DK3 Walter.

S-5 DIVISION:
Kept the three wardrooms running efficiently.

Lt.j.g. Randall.

SD3 Alexander, TN Aquino, TN Bailey, SD3 Black, TN
Boykins, TN Burns, TN Cain, TN Campbell, SD1
Castile, SD3 Castro, SD2 Castro, TN Coleman, TN
Cruz, TN Dancy, SD3 Delfin, SD3 Dumlao, SD2 Duty,
TN Earl, SD2 Edwards, SD3 Fernandez, TN Foster,
SD3 Gastilo, SD3 Gonzales, TN Gooding, SD2 Hall,
SD2 Hall, TN Harris, TN Hassell, TN Hilson, TN Hol-
land, SD2 Hoosier, TN Igno, SD1 Johnson, TN John-

(Navy Photo by PH1 P. D. Goodrich)

son, TN Jones, SD3 Ladson, TN Lagarejos, SD1
Lewis, SD1 McCargo, SD1 McCoy, TN McClendon, TN
McDonald, SD3 Manila, SD3 Mariano, SD1 Mingo, TN
Owens, TN Pareles, SD3 Profeta, TN Pusalan, SD3
Reid, TN Reyes, SD1 Riley, TN Robinson, SD3
Salazar, TN Scott, TN Scott, SD3 Sherman, SD3 Sims,
TN Sims, TN Singleton, SD3 Stanton, SD3 Stevenson,
SKSN Taxer, SD3 Taylor, SD1 Tiamanglo, SD3 Todd,
TN Trapela, SD3 Tyson, TN Vanlue, TN Vega, TN
Williams, TN Wynn.

S-6 DIVISION:
Maintained spare parts for the aircraft.

Lt. j.g. Merrick, AKC Wilhelm.

AN Adams, AK1 Baumgartner, AKAN Danish, AN
Defeo, AN Dukes, AN Engelbert, AN Evans, AK1
Gibson, AN Greene, AN Groat, AK2 Hayes, AK1
Holley, AK2 Hollowood, AK3 Ingold, AN Johnson, AN
Kopydlowski, AK2 Loyd, AK3 Mason, AN Milks, AN
Muntz, AKAN Nelson, AK2 Noller, AK2 Owens, AN
Peavey, AK3 Penyok, AK2 Rheaume, AK3 Robbins,
AK3 Sheets, AK2 Swaim, AN Szparkowski, AN Willett,
AK2 Young.

The USS *Saratoga* Supporters

The following individuals and organizations made a contribution to see the USS *Saratoga* made into a naval museum in Jacksonville, Florida, and to the success of this book.

Barbara A. Anderson
Arko Industrial Group
Atlantic Firebrick & Supply Co.
Ross V. Beedle
LCDR James R. Beeler
John E. Burke
Shirley A. Burke
Michael F. Charland
The Cleaning Cubans, Inc.
Barry D. Collins
Bob Coffey
Computax by Pioneer F/S
LCDR Wallace J. Conway, USNRET
Melissa Cook
1st Class Petty Officer Bryon Crosby
George and Wanda Czechlewski
Chief Vincent Darrigo
Pat Daugherty
Lana R. Dazey
Charles and Mervin Denny
Jim Douglas
Donald D. Downs
James L. Dudley
Ronald J. Eisenberg
LCDR Bill Farnsworth, USN (RTD)
Herbert Feinman
George Ferrara
Ken J. Finegan
Laura S. Franklin
Guy Austin Gay
Larry Gordon
Warren Grymes
Ernie Haakenson
Robert F. Hackman
O. J. Harding
Paul J. Hartung
Lewis Holden
David N. Holton
Donald Howe

Rita M. Hubbs
Sandra G. Hughes
Integrated Environmental Solutions, Inc.
Capt. Brent S. James
RADM Jack M. James
Don Jeffers
Jim Baker Corporation
John W. Johnson, II
Bill O. Johnson
AMCS (AW) J. J. Jones, Jr.
Pete Keenan
Capt. William Kennedy
Corporal Jonathan D. Kern
Robert Kingston
Charles Knight
Valdemar G. Lambert
Language Bank International
Lee & Cates Glass, Inc.
Liberty Bail Bonds, Inc.
Walter R. Lockwood, Sr.
Brad Long
Pam & Joshua C. Mancillas
Guy Marvin
RADM Alfred R. Matter
LCDR David N. Maynard
George G. Mayzell, M.D.
Tom McCabe
Joseph McCloskey
Major Charles R. Mehle, II, U.S. Army
Lance R. Mehle
RADM and Mrs. Roger W. Mehle
Lloyd P. Miller
Naughton Insurance Services, Inc.
Louis V. Negrelli
Orange Park Adult Specialty Care, P.A.
Francis A. Packer, Jr. (Cdr. USN Ret.)

L. C. Page, Jr.
William P. Patterson
Hiron H. Peck, Inc.
Andy Phillips
Thomas Plitt and Jodi Stahl
C. Edward Powell
Robert S. Powell
Tom Quinn
Vice Admiral John K. Ready, USN (Ret.)
Robert Ready
Wayne Rickert
Marlene and Harry V. Roberts, Jr.
Lt. Darin Rogers
Steve Rudin
Roger A. Ruis
Henry W. Ryan, Jr.
VADM & Mrs. James R. Sanderson
Brad Senter
Donna M. Setaro
Sidney H. Showalter
James D. Small, Capt. USN (Ret.)
Paul C. Stadler
Rick and Rebecca Stein
Joe Stelma
Col. William H. Tomlinson, USA (Ret.)
Richard A. Toppings
Peter S. Tuggle
Capt. J. M. Tully, Jr.
Joe Turgeon
United States Marine Drill Instructors Association
David S. Walker
Sherrill A. Weber
James Whalen
Gordon Wileen
Jerry Wisner
Constantino Zarate
Robert J. Zarse

Acknowledgments

Special thanks to Longstreet Press editor Scott E. Czechlewski, who directed the project from its inception, providing invaluable guidance and editing expertise.

And special thanks to Lieutenant John M. Wallach, who served as *Saratoga*'s Public Affairs Officer on the ship's final deployment. His assistance was invaluable in both text and photograph research.

THE FOLLOWING ORGANIZATIONS AND INDIVIDUALS PROVIDED PHOTOGRAPHS AND RELATED ASSISTANCE:

Russell D. Egnor, Director News Photo Division, Navy
    Office of Information
Chief Richard Toppings, Chief of Naval Information,
    News Photograph Division
Charles Haberlein
Ed Finney, Jr.
Photographic Section of the Curator Branch of the
    Naval Historical Center
Saratoga Photo Boss Ensign Brian Lee
PH1 Lawrence Emil Seehafer
All photographers on board the *Saratoga* whose work
    went into the collection of available Navy
    photographs

Ernie Haakenson
Harvey Hirsch, USS *Saratoga* Association
Tony Tonelli, USS *Saratoga* Association
George Tanis
Patricia Mehle
Stephen D. Tanner
Edward Griffin
Donald Howe
Patrick Broderick
John Merserve
Larry Gordon
James Whalen
Julius L. Evans, JO1, USN

THE FOLLOWING ORGANIZATIONS, INDIVIDUALS AND PUBLICATIONS PROVIDED INVALUABLE BACKGROUND AND RELATED ASSISTANCE:

Ship's History branch of the Naval Historical Center and the sailors throughout *Saratoga*'s career who compiled the Command Histories.

Harvey Palmer, librarian Mayport Naval Station
Lieutenant Commander Dave Maynard
The Dictionary of American Naval Fighting Ships,
    Volume VI, 1976, Naval History Division, Depart-
    ment of the Navy.
*Aircraft Carriers of the World, 1914 to the Present,
    An Illustrated Encyclopedia*, Roger Chesneau,
    Naval Institute Press.
Jane's Fighting Ships, 96th Edition, 1993-1994, Jane's
    information Group Limited, Sentinel House.
The Hook (Summer 1980) "USS *Saratoga* (CV-60)"
    by Robert L. Broaddus & Robert Cressman.
In Peace And War: Interpretations of American Naval

History, 1775-1978. Edited by Kenneth J. Hagan,
    Greenwood Press, Westport, Conn./London, England.
    1978.
The American Fighter, by Enzo Angelucci, consultant
    Peter M. Bowers. Orion Books, New York. 1985.
U.S. War Birds from World War I to Vietnam, Kenneth
    Munson, New Orchard Editions, 1985.
The Florida Times-Union
Newsweek
The New York Times
The New York Daily News
The New York Herald Tribune
The Philadelphia Inquirer

THE FOLLOWING REPRESENTATIVES OF JACKSONVILLE, FLORIDA, AND OF THE JACKSONVILLE CHAMBER OF COMMERCE PROVIDED INVALUABLE ASSISTANCE IN THE CREATION OF THIS BOOK:

Tillie Fowler, U.S. Congress representative for Jacksonville
Don Davis, Jacksonville City Council President
Charles Sawyer, Jacksonville Transportation Authority Chairman
Susan Milhoan, Vice President of Communications and Membership, Jacksonville Chamber of Commerce
Jay Mooney, Jacksonville Chamber of Commerce Beaches Development Department
Dave Stevens

Index